"The fact is, I'm very strongly attracted to you. I want to take you places, show you things, make you laugh, kiss you until you can't stand up."

Chelsea's eyes widened. She felt a flush climb her cheeks.

"I think the only answer is to cancel the contract, which will leave us free to see each other without any confusing complications," Jeff said. Chelsea tried to swallow, but her throat was too dry.

"I can't," she said hoarsely.

"Of course you can. We both know that what happened on the beach this morning wasn't accidental. It was inevitable. I'm surprised it didn't happen sooner. The chemistry between us is extraordinary." She couldn't believe he was saying these things; she'd never heard a man talk so bluntly about his feelings. It aroused her, opened something inside her. For a long, vulnerable moment, she even was tempted to throw herself into his arms. Instead, Chelsea forced her mouth into a polite smile.

"I'm sorry, but I can't. You see, I'm engaged."

St. Martin's Paperbacks Titles by Amy Belding Brown

ISLAND SUMMER LOVE
STRAWBERRY LACE

Strawberry Lace

AMY BELDING BROWN

ST. MARTIN'S PAPERBACKS

STRAWBERRY LACE

ISBN: 0-312-95327-5

Printed in the United States of America

St. Martin's Paperbacks edition/October 1994

10 9 8 7 6 5 4 3 2 1

Chapter One

WHEN CHELSEA RECEIVED THE REQUEST in mid-May to cater Muriel Winter's Independence Day buffet, she almost said no. It was her first reaction, an automatic, almost instinctive response. In fact, if it had been Muriel who called, instead of her personal secretary, she would have refused on the spot. But Beth Harmon's warmly efficient voice made her pause just long enough to consider the possibilities. Muriel Winter's parties were attended by the wealthiest summer people in southern Maine. Chelsea knew it would be an incredible opportunity for her fledgling catering business, one she couldn't afford to pass up.

She accepted with just the slightest edge of bitterness in her voice. "Strawberry Lace is always glad to welcome new clients. May I ask how Mrs. Winter selected us?"

"She was disappointed with her last caterer," Beth said. "She's been looking around. Someone mentioned your name. Are you familiar with the Winter estate?"

"I was there once, several years ago. I don't remember many details." Chelsea's mind flickered darkly and she tugged at a strand of her strawberry-blond hair to remind herself this was a business call. No time for dragging up old grievances. "I'd like to come up and take a look around, if that's possible."

"Of course. You name the time."

"How about tomorrow?" Chelsea squinted at her calendar. "I'm free at eleven."

"That would be fine. Come to the service entrance. I'll meet you there."

Chelsea penciled in the appointment and circled the fourth of July on the big wall calendar before she called Lori. She knew her older sister would be thrilled at the prospect of doing the Winter party. None of Chelsea's resentment had ever rubbed off on her.

But then, Lori wasn't Holly Martin's best friend. She hadn't gone through weeks and weeks of sympathetic anguish as Holly struggled to recover from her broken engagement with Brandon Winter. It had taken almost six months. Six months of watching Holly fade away to skin and bones because she stopped eating. Six months of listening to her cry every time they talked. Six months of fighting her own growing indignation, before Holly finally decided she had to leave Maine and get as far away as possible from Muriel Winter and her East Coast money. So now Holly was living in Los Angeles. Chelsea hadn't seen her in over a year, and she wasn't likely to either. Because Holly still hadn't gotten over Brandon.

And it was all Muriel Winter's doing. She had taken one look at Holly and decided she wasn't good enough for her son. Decided that Holly's slim, dark-eyed beauty and her generous, loving personality counted for nothing. All that mattered was that the Martin family didn't have money or culture, that they didn't come from the social elite, that they weren't summer people, but fishermen. At his mother's insistence, Brandon had broken the engagement one hot August afternoon on the Winters' private beach. And almost three years of Holly's devotion to the tall, handsome financier had been trashed. Just like that.

Chelsea still couldn't think about it without seething. She vividly recalled Holly's phone call the night of the breakup. Her friend had been close to hysteria, her breathing so rapid and loud that Chelsea could hear the gasps over the phone. She'd dropped everything and rushed over to Holly's apartment, where she'd spent all night trying to calm her down. Holly was still wearing her engagement ring then, the huge heart-shaped solitaire shimmering on her left hand, and Chelsea had kept looking at it and wanting to pull it off her finger and flush it down the toilet. But when she suggested that Holly remove it, her friend had vehemently refused. She'd worn the ring for weeks afterward, until Chelsea finally told her how pathetic it looked.

Holly had glanced down at her hand and smiled faintly. "You're right. It is pathetic. And so am I." She slid it off her finger and dropped it into Chelsea's hand. "You take it."

"Me? No, Holly—come on." Chelsea tried to hand it back to her and then thought better of it. "What am I supposed to do with it?"

Holly shrugged. "I don't know. Sell it. Buy yourself a new van for the business."

Chelsea still had the ring, locked in a safe deposit box down at Merchant's Bank. She was resolved to keep it and give it back to Holly when she finally got over Brandon Winter. If that day ever came.

She shook herself out of her memories and reached for the phone. Lori answered on the fifth ring.

"Guess what, sis?" She made her voice bright. There was no point in sending bad vibes over the phone. Not when her sister was seven months pregnant with her first baby. "We just got a big one."

"The Gables?" Lori sounded excited already.

"Even bigger. Muriel Winter's Independence Day party."

"You're kidding! Muriel *Winter?*"

"No joke. I'm going up there tomorrow to look the place over. Want to come along?"

"Of course! I wouldn't miss it!"

"Great." Chelsea brushed at a lemon-colored stain on her apron. "I'll pick you up at ten-thirty."

Chelsea was wearing her trademark pink lace blouse and brushed-denim skirt when she picked Lori up in the van. For three years now she'd used the van almost exclusively. It wasn't just that her little red Toyota was on its last legs, but driving the van around Maynard Landing, even into Portland, was just good business sense. The dark blue Dodge with its logo of a wicker basket trailing strawberry vines and streamers of lace was advertising, after all. She'd painted it herself after weeks of laboring over the design, had lettered the words STRAWBERRY LACE carefully over the logo, with the phrase *Catering to the Cream of the Coast* written in a long, lacy curve underneath. She had never been entirely pleased with the motto. It seemed a bit too pretentious, but Lori and her husband Paul had loved it, and, as Paul pointed out, it was too risky from a business perspective to change it now.

The business had done quite well, growing by word of mouth over the past three years, drawing most of its clientele from professional upper-middle-class couples who worked in Portland and lived in the beautiful little coastal towns nearby. It had yet to insinuate its way into the wealthy summer population, but perhaps now that would change. They would just have to keep their fingers crossed and hope all went well.

"I'm going to have nightmares about this for weeks," Lori said as she settled herself into the passenger seat and strapped her seat belt over her swollen waist. "From what I've heard, Muriel Winter is the kind of person who notices everything. One detail out of place, and we're dead."

"We have to think positively." Chelsea swung out of Lori's driveway and headed up the hill out of Maynard Landing. The Winter estate was thirty minutes away, at the end of a long, winding road off Route 1. You drove for miles through pine forest, thinking the road must be taking you all the way to Portland, until the woods suddenly opened up and you could see the house, high on a rise overlooking the sea. It was huge, large enough to be an inn: a rambling, two-story, white clapboard building with deep porches and wide, sloping lawns, the grass so luxuriantly thick it felt like velvet under your feet. At the foot of the lawns was the ocean, which rolled constantly onto a crescent of sand beach, tucked between high rocky ledges.

"I wonder if we'll actually get to see Muriel herself," said Lori. "Maybe she'll want to meet us."

"I doubt it," Chelsea said. "If so, it'll just be to look

us over. See if we're presentable. From what I've heard, she has a secret suspicion that all Maine natives are ignorant, bumbling fools."

"You're thinking about her attitude toward Holly."

Chelsea nodded. "The one time I was invited to a cocktail party as Holly's friend, Queen Muriel didn't even introduce herself to me. She was too busy holding court for all the yacht owners. They have boats that they can't operate without a crew, but they all think they're sailors."

Lori chuckled. "For the sake of the business, I hope we don't meet her. One look at you smoldering away and she'll cancel the deal."

"You're right." Chelsea slowed the van and turned right onto Route 1. She glanced at her sister and smiled. Lori was sitting with her hands cupped over the swell of her belly, a bemused expression on her beautiful oval face. "I promise, I'll behave myself."

Chelsea followed the gravel driveway all the way around to the back of the house and parked at the service entrance. She scowled through the windshield, surveying the heavy wooden door. Talk about pretentious. It looked as if it had been acquired directly from an English castle. It was overhung with ivy, which had clearly been trained to grow over the thick stones of the building's foundation. A flagstone terrace flanked by low shrubs was tucked into a small recess to the door's right. As she got out of the van, she spotted a cluster of tennis courts on a ridge of land to their left, and beyond them, a low, gray building that could only be a riding stable.

"Wow!" Lori circled the van to join her. "I had no idea it was so elegant! This is like a palace! Do you think we'll get a complete tour?"

"One way or the other. If we're not shown the whole place, we'll use one of our undercover techniques." Chelsea grinned at her sister. "We might as well get started." She crossed the parking lot to the door and knocked twice before she spotted the bell, hidden under a cluster of ivy leaves.

She was reaching for it when the door opened suddenly and Chelsea found herself looking up into a pair of the darkest, most attractive eyes she'd ever seen.

"Oh, hello." She was abruptly, oddly flustered. The man in front of her was incredibly handsome, with the chiseled, regular features you usually saw only in magazine ads. He looked a few years older than she, perhaps in his early thirties. Damp strands of black hair hung over his forehead. A lower lip slightly fuller than his upper one gave him an intensely sensual aura. He was wearing faded blue jeans and a worn white T-shirt, through which she could clearly see the tight undulation of his well-developed muscles. There was a tiny gold stud in his left ear, and, she noticed, as she glanced down in a vain attempt to recover her equilibrium, his feet were bare.

"May I help you?" The owner of the eyes smiled down at her.

Chelsea took a small step backward. "We're from Strawberry Lace."

The man's smile disappeared; he gave her a blank look.

"The catering service."

"And?"

"We have an eleven o'clock appointment with Miss Harmon."

"Oh, yeah." The smile returned, broadened into a

grin; a deep, curving dimple appeared in his left cheek. "Beth did mention something about a meeting. Hang on, I'll get her." He disappeared briefly, leaving Chelsea and Lori standing at the open door.

Lori chuckled. "Who do you figure he is—the butler?"

Chelsea shrugged. "Maybe the chauffeur. The butler wouldn't leave us standing here, would he?"

The man returned. "Sorry to keep you waiting. Come on in. Beth'll be right with you." His eyes were shining with laughter.

Chelsea followed him into a wide room with high ceilings and dark wood paneling. It was empty, except for a counter that ran the length of one wall.

The man was still smiling and watching her with those disturbing eyes. Chelsea tried to make herself smile back at him, but her face felt wooden and stiff.

"Sorry I can't offer you a place to sit." He shrugged and opened his hands. "Would you like to wait in the kitchen?" Chelsea noted his long fingers.

"We're fine," Lori said.

The man's eyes flicked over to her briefly, then settled again on Chelsea, who felt a distinct wave of relief a moment later, when Beth Harmon came rushing through a door at the far end of the room. Her short, curly hair was damp and her face was flushed. Her clothes looked hastily put on. Chelsea shot a quick glance back at the man. His eyes had shifted, and he was now watching Beth with an appreciative smile. Chelsea held out her hand.

"Miss Harmon? I'm Chelsea Adams and this is Lori LeBlanc."

Beth shook their hands warmly. "Please call me Beth. I see you've already met Jeff."

"Only informally." The man was suddenly beside

Beth, extending his hand toward Chelsea. "Jeff Blaine." He wrapped his fingers around hers. "At your service."

Chelsea was startled to find herself blushing. It was something about the way he was looking at her, the intensity of his gaze, as if he were mentally stripping her. She nodded quickly, withdrew her hand and turned to Beth. "I'm looking forward to seeing the grounds."

"Of course. I'm sorry if I kept you waiting."

"No problem." Actually, it was good to know that Muriel Winter's servants had lives of their own, that working in the big house sometimes had its moments of pleasure.

The tour started in the kitchen. Beth pushed a button on the entryway wall and two sections of paneling slid open to reveal an enormous kitchen. Lori gasped with delight, and even Chelsea couldn't contain her excitement.

"This is wonderful!" She ran her hand over one of the three, long, polished wood counters. The walls were faced in aged red bricks and divided by multipaned windows. Rows of polished brass pendant lights hung over the counters. Pots, pans, and ladles hung from a latticework of beams between the counters. Chelsea glanced out one window into a small, informal garden bounded by hedges which, she saw, were actually thick rosebushes. A stone birdbath and two white-painted, wrought-iron benches were surrounded by a profusion of ferns and flowers. She imagined herself sitting on one of the benches, reading or just enjoying the colors and smells. What would it feel like to live in a place like this, with so much luxury and beauty available always?

Lori's hand on her shoulder pulled her out of her reverie and she turned to find Beth opening another door.

"This is the pantry." Beth swept her hand through the doorway, inviting them to explore the long, narrow room. It was filled to the ceiling with ancient, glass-walled cupboards. "You're welcome to use all the space you need, of course," Beth said. "Mrs. Winter's only requirement is that it's left in the condition in which it was found."

"That won't be a problem," said Chelsea crisply. "We always clean up after an affair."

Beth nodded. "Mrs. Winter thoroughly investigated your reputation before she chose Strawberry Lace. She doesn't enjoy taking chances." She turned back to the kitchen.

Chelsea rolled her eyes at Lori, who gave her an admonishing frown and gestured toward Beth, who was still speaking.

"Mrs. Winter wants the party centered on the lawn directly off the dining room. I'll show you."

Chelsea glanced again toward the pantry. "Does Mrs. Winter prefer that we use her serving pieces or shall we provide our own?"

Beth gave her a startled look. "Mrs. Winter *always* uses her own. She wouldn't have it any other way."

"Then I'll need to take some more time in the kitchen area."

"Of course." Beth seemed agitated, impatient. "Let me finish the tour first and then you can take all the time you need." Beth led the way to a door at the far end of the kitchen.

Chelsea swallowed a smile. Beth clearly wanted to get the tour over with, so she could get back to Jeff. She couldn't blame her either. There had been something about him, beyond his amazing good looks, that would excite any red-blooded American woman. He was alive in a way that had made her own skin tingle just being in the same room with him.

She followed Lori and Beth up a narrow flight of stairs to the dining room. Like the kitchen, it was huge, dominated by a long walnut table and antique Chippendale chairs centered on the shining, parquet floor. It was papered in pale mint; one long wall was given over to a row of French doors which opened onto a flagstone patio and the sloping lawn beyond.

Beth waved her hand in the direction of the ocean. "There should be a tent set up on the lawn to accommodate the guests in case of rain. Is that something you can arrange?"

"Of course."

"Good." Beth smiled. With relief, Chelsea thought. Probably if they hadn't been able to provide a tent, she would have had to arrange for it. And a million other little details.

"I assume she'd like cocktails first?" Lori asked.

"Yes, at about four o'clock, with dinner starting no later than seven. Buffet-style, unless it rains, in which case it should be sit-down." Beth crossed to a door on the wall opposite the windows. "In here are a couple of smaller dining rooms. You may use them if you think it's necessary."

Chelsea checked out the two smaller rooms. One had a fireplace and a small, round dining table. Blue and green chintz fabric decorated the upholstered chairs. It was a perfect place to set up a dessert buffet. She slipped her notebook out of her purse and started writing. Her best ideas often attacked her when she was on the premises, and it wasn't always easy to remember them later. She wrote furiously, only vaguely aware of Lori's string of routine questions. Lori was the detail person, the one who made sure all the questions were asked, all the fussy particulars organized. This allowed Chelsea to let her mind run wild, which was the real secret to their success. They were creative and careful at the same time, a rare combination. Chelsea looked up from her notebook to find Lori and Beth standing in the doorway to the main dining room.

"Mrs. Winter doesn't approve of music at her parties," Beth was saying. "She claims it drowns out the ocean."

Lori made sympathetic noises. "And you said there would be about sixty guests?"

"Yes, that's a pretty firm figure. Almost everyone attends who's lucky enough to be invited to one of Mrs. Winter's parties."

Chelsea tasted something bitter in the back of her throat.

"I'll show you part of the grounds now," Beth continued. "Unfortunately, there are certain gardens that are off-limits. Mrs. Winter is very particular about her gardens." She crossed the parquet floor to open one of the French doors. A cool sea breeze swirled into the room.

"Excuse me," Chelsea said, "but if you don't mind, I'd like to check out the kitchen again." She smiled apologetically and waved them on. "You go ahead, Lori. I'll catch up with you."

This was an old tactic; they'd used it so many times, Lori didn't even miss a beat.

"That's a great idea, Chels," she said, taking Beth's

arm and steering her outside before Muriel Winter's personal secretary had the chance to consider the implications of an outsider wandering unaccompanied through the big house.

Chapter Two

CHELSEA DUCKED THROUGH THE DOOR and hurried back down the stairs. She did need to check out the kitchen again, so she hadn't actually lied. But it was more than that. The reason she always invented an excuse to be alone in the house where they were going to cater a party was to get a sense of the building's vibrations. It was a weird idea, one she knew no employer would understand, least of all an arrogant one like Muriel Winter. But it was important to pick up the emanations of the house, to detect the "warm" spots in the building, where people were most likely to relax and open up to each other. It was the real secret ingredient of their success, the reason that Strawberry Lace had yet to cater a party where the guests hadn't gone home raving about the food.

She promised herself to take no more than twenty minutes. After quickly checking out the kitchen, making sure that the requisite number of trays and chafing dishes was available, she slipped back up the stairs to thoroughly explore the first floor. Off the main dining room were the two smaller dining rooms, overlooking an expansive rose garden. Off the larger of these two rooms was a small kitchen. She mentally berated Beth for not revealing this room, then reasoned that it was probably used privately by the Winter family—though she couldn't imagine Muriel Winter lifting a finger anywhere near a stove—and Beth had probably had orders not to show it. Still, it would be a useful place from which to serve the hot hors d'oeuvres. She made a note to ask Beth about its availability for the party. She'd beg if she had to. At the very least, she'd point out how much more successful a party was if the waiters weren't exhausted from running up and downstairs.

Most of the cooking would be done outdoors, in the long grills she'd had made to specification. The hors d'oeuvres would be made ahead of time, which only left the preparation of the dessert sauces for the fruit mélange, the baking of the shortcake, and whipping the cream to be done on the premises. They would use the long dining table as a buffet table, with their trademark of fresh strawberries mounded in a lace-draped wicker basket as the centerpiece.

She noted that the smallest dining room was a definite warm spot. She could feel the little hairs on the back of her neck lift in excitement. She would definitely use this room for something. If she could get people in here first thing, it would start the party off on the right foot. They'd be feeling great before the main meal was even served.

Chelsea tucked the notebook back into her purse and crossed to the far end of the big dining room, where an open doorway led to a hallway. She peeked into a sitting room and caught a glimpse of pastel-blue walls, white woodwork and blue and rose chintz, a stack of magazines on a walnut coffee table.

She noted the warm tingling at the top of her spine. Another warm spot. Something to keep in mind.

She checked her watch, realized that she was already pushing her self-imposed twenty-minute time limit. She glanced quickly into a powder room, a dark-paneled, book-filled library, and then she came to the main living room.

It was gorgeous. There wasn't any other word for it. It ran the entire length of the house, yet the clever arrangement of comfortable furniture made it look inviting and homelike, almost cozy. Someone had decorated it with a sure, practiced hand. Pale blue walls and white woodwork, fireplaces at each end, blue and white upholstered chairs and couches, and an exquisite Aubusson carpet, made it definitely the most beautiful room in the house.

Tall windows looked out on a deep porch, facing the ocean. Light filtered through trees at the side windows, scattering blue and gold patterns across the floor. She imagined herself sitting here on a late summer afternoon, tucked into a corner of a couch, reading a book, or talking quietly with her good friend Stuart. Everything was serene and graceful, with an understated elegance that was almost erotic in its intensity. The image was almost too powerful to resist. She took a deep breath and smiled. Another warm spot, definitely. It was too bad Muriel Winter hadn't decided that this room would be the party center. She looked at her watch again and scowled. She's taken almost thirty minutes, much too long. She'd have to go hunting for Lori and Beth now, and make up some story about counting the spoons to cover herself.

She hurried back to the dining room and went out through the French doors. She shaded her eyes to scrutinize the sweeping lawns. There was no sign of either Beth or Lori. She shrugged. She'd start by circling the house and keeping her ears open. She could recognize the sound of her big sister's voice a mile away.

Chelsea headed for a gap in the shrubbery to her left, and within minutes she was lost in a maze of gardens. She didn't panic at first, reasoning that she could always retrace her steps. But uneasiness turned to anxiety as she tried to get her bearings and pushed through a thick hedge of rosebushes, ripping her panty hose and tearing a line of tiny holes in her skirt.

She groaned and collapsed onto a wrought-iron bench. She was bending over her skirt, cursing herself for her clumsiness, when she heard a movement behind her. She jumped to her feet and whirled, only to find herself looking, once again, into the dark eyes of Jeff Blaine.

He was wearing the same jeans and white T-shirt, only now he had a red bandanna knotted around his head and his feet were no longer bare. He was wearing cowboy boots, expensive ones, she noted, which seemed strangely incongruous in this manicured setting. He held a pair of garden shears and he was grinning at her, that same, unsettling grin he'd given her before.

"Well, well, what have we here? Snooping around the house all by ourselves, are we?"

"No! Of course not! I was looking for Beth and Lori. I seem to have gotten lost. These gardens are confusing."

He nodded, still grinning, as he came toward her. There was a smear of dirt across the front of his

T-shirt, and sweat had dampened the bandanna. He was obviously the gardener.

"Would you mind showing me the way back to the house?" Chelsea tried furtively to cover the rip in her skirt by draping one arm in front of her, but she saw that it was too late; his eyes had spotted the tear.

"You didn't hurt yourself did you? Those roses are killers."

"I'm fine. Just take me back to the house, Mr. Blaine."

"Jeff," he said. "And I'd be happy to help you. I'm always delighted to rescue a lady in distress." He tossed the garden shears onto the bench. "This particular area is a loosely designed maze, so stay close." Without another word, he took her hand and led her along a narrow, twisting path between tall, yellow flowers she didn't recognize.

She couldn't believe how awkward she felt. She wasn't the kind of woman to get lost in the first place; she had a keen sense of direction. She rarely even had to rely on maps to locate where she was going. Yet here she was, lost only a few feet from a house, in a garden so huge it was like some giant's labyrinth. To top it all off, a disconcertingly handsome gardener with the most extraordinary eyes she'd ever seen was leading her by the hand as if she were a baby.

She was trying to figure out how to remove her hand without offending the gardener, when he parted some shrubbery and they were suddenly standing at a corner of the wide front porch.

"There." He released her with a firm squeeze. "All safe and sound."

"Thank you very much." She knew she sounded uncharacteristically prim, but she couldn't help it.

She hadn't felt so unnerved in years. "I really appreciate it."

"Hey, no problem. How about a glass of lemonade or something?"

"Thanks, but I couldn't."

"Sure you could. Come on, we'll wait for Beth in the kitchen." He turned away and headed off along another path close to the house.

Chelsea hesitated a moment, then went after him. She was struck by how charismatic he was; she found it hard to resist his suggestions. It was almost as if his eyes had hypnotized her. She understood how easy it must have been for him to seduce Beth Harmon. One wink from this man could, she suspected, melt most women.

Luckily, she was immune to such maneuvers. Her long-term relationship with Stuart Potter protected her from an interest in other men. She'd been friends with Stuart since high school, when they'd discovered a mutual passion for the ocean. Though Chelsea had never pursued that obsession the way Stuart had when he went into business as a lobsterman, she still loved the times when they took off in his boat for leisurely explorations of the Casco Bay islands. There was nothing better than lounging on the deck of *Chelsea's Choice* on a cloudless, summer afternoon.

Chelsea had been flattered when Stuart named his boat after her, and when some of her friends had attached a romantic significance to the gesture, she'd wondered if maybe Stuart *was* trying to tell her something. It had never occurred to her that Stuart might think of her as anything other than a close friend. But perhaps there were undercurrents in their relationship she wasn't aware of.

Anyhow, she was much too happy with things as they were to want to make changes. She knew that most people assumed she and Stuart were lovers, and she'd never gone out of her way to correct the illusion. Letting them think she had an active sex life had its advantages. People introduced her to their single male friends with a certain tone in their voices which conveyed the understanding that she was taken. When she was approached at a party by some obnoxious man, all she had to do was mention Stuart's name. She never had to worry about whether she'd be spending Saturday night alone; she never agonized over finding an escort to the dances she loved. Stuart was always there for her. They had the kind of warm, secure, comfortable relationship that most couples didn't achieve until after years of marriage. There were no emotional demands between them. They were just good friends. It was a perfect relationship.

Chelsea rarely discussed these thoughts with anyone but Stuart; she knew without inquiring that other people would object. The myth that chemistry was the most important aspect of a male-female relationship was deeply ingrained in the culture. But except for a brief fling in college with an egotistical teaching assistant, she'd gotten along just fine for twenty-six years without passion. There was a lot more to life than hormones. Her own mother's failed marriages certainly proved that romance wasn't all it was cracked up to be.

Jeff's voice pulled her back into the present. "Come on in," he said, opening a door to reveal the big, brick-walled kitchen. "Make yourself at home." He crossed the huge room and took a pitcher of lemonade from one of the big refrigerators. "Glasses are in the cupboard in the pantry. First one on your left, second shelf."

Chelsea found two tall blue tumblers and set them on the kitchen counter. Jeff was at the sink, washing his hands.

"So how'd you get into the catering business?" he asked over his shoulder.

"Actually, it was a friend's idea. About three years ago we were both going crazy in our jobs in Portland, and she suggested that we start our own business. It took about two minutes to come up with the idea of catering; we both loved to cook."

He grabbed a towel from a rack beside the sink and turned to face her. "Loved? As in past tense?"

"No, not at all. I couldn't be happier."

He dried his hands and flipped the towel back onto the rack. "I couldn't help noticing that your friend is pregnant."

"Oh, Lori's not my friend, she's my sister." Chelsea slid onto one of the tall stools beside the counter. "My friend's gone. She's been living in L.A. for the past two years."

He poured lemonade into the glasses and handed her one as he sat on the stool beside her. She was surprised at the strange flutter in her stomach. It wasn't at all like her to react to a man's proximity. She took a sip of lemonade. It was delicious, just the right mixture of sweetness and tartness. She wondered if she dared ask him to get the recipe for her.

"Why L.A.?" Jeff was holding his glass in front of his chin, staring at her over the rim.

"Because she wanted to get as far away from the East Coast as possible." Chelsea pushed a stray lock of hair behind her ear and took another sip.

"Why?"

The man was full of questions. And he was still watching her; he hadn't even tasted his lemonade. Chelsea wondered how much she should say about Holly's situation, then decided to go ahead and tell him what had happened. He wouldn't be surprised; he worked for Muriel Winter himself and he surely knew her customs.

"Because the Winter family lives on the East Coast. She was engaged to Mrs. Winter's son, Brandon. And then your employer"—Chelsea rolled her eyes—"got on her high horse and broke it up. My friend wasn't good enough for her wonderful son." She took another swallow of lemonade, letting the tangy liquid wash her suddenly dry throat. "Holly's heart was broken. She almost killed herself. But she's better now. At least in L.A. she isn't always reading in the paper about the Winter family's latest financial maneuvers."

Jeff put down his glass and shifted closer to her. His mouth was quirked into a strange little grin; his dark eyes were shining. "So you don't have much admiration for Mrs. Winter, I take it?"

"That's putting it mildly. I know she's very popular with the rich crowd along the coast. But I don't know any regular people who respect her." She swung on her stool to face him. "Do you like working for her?"

He shrugged. "She's not so bad."

"Well, to each his own, I guess." She found refuge again in her lemonade, taking a long drink. She'd obviously made a mistake, telling the gardener her feelings about Muriel Winter. He probably hadn't been working for her long enough to glimpse her ruthless side.

"What do you do for fun, Chelsea?" He was still

watching her. She could feel the pressure of his eyes, almost as if they were the pads of his fingers, firm and hot on her skin.

"To tell you the truth, I don't have a lot of free time." She glanced at her watch. "I wonder where Lori is? She should be done by now."

"She'll be along any minute. What's the hurry?" He reached out and brushed her arm with his finger. "Are you free this afternoon?"

"Why?"

"I thought maybe we could spend it together."

Her stomach fluttered again. It was such an odd, disturbing sensation, like hundreds of insects flying around inside her. "Doing what?" The question came out so spontaneously, she didn't even think about its implication until he smiled. Then she realized that she'd given him a conditional assent, that by not saying no immediately, she'd given him the impression that she was willing, that it was simply a matter of finding some mutually agreeable activity.

He touched her arm again, very lightly. "We could go to the beach. It's a nice, warm day."

"I can't. I have too much to do. Don't you have to work?"

He smiled. "I'm free all afternoon. The evening too, if that's better. How about dinner?"

She shook her head and slid her arm away from him. "I really can't."

"Another time maybe."

"Well, no. Actually, I'm involved with someone."

His face sobered briefly. "I can't say I'm surprised. Though I am disappointed." He picked up his glass and took a long drink.

Chelsea got up and crossed the room to one of the windows. Perhaps she should go out and look for

Lori and Beth. The risk of getting lost again seemed minuscule compared to the discomfort of being in the same room with this seductive gardener. She could understand why Beth had looked as she did when she and Lori first arrived. If he came on to Beth the same way he had to her just now, it would be next to impossible to resist him. The thought jarred her, and she tasted a film of disgust on the back of her tongue. How could she even *think* such a thing? She'd learned long ago that there was nobody out there who could come close to offering her the warm companionship she had with Stuart. She sent up a silent prayer of thanksgiving for her friend.

She was about to open the door and look around when she heard Lori's voice and the sound of footsteps on the stairs to the dining room. She felt a wave of grateful relief as she turned to greet her sister.

Beth was showing them out to the van when Chelsea suddenly remembered the flowers. She kicked herself for having forgotten them; it was always important to know what the client preferred in the way of floral arrangements. Usually it was one of the first things she covered after seeing the layout. Obviously, the encounter with the gardener had unsettled her even more than she realized.

She turned to Beth, who was shaking Lori's hand. "I'm afraid I've forgotten something." She smiled awkwardly. "I assume Mrs. Winter wants floral arrangements."

"Of course. And she'll want her own flowers used for the party. She's very particular about that."

Chelsea nodded. No surprise. "Particular" was the understatement of the year. Mrs. Winter was the most particular person she'd ever laid eyes on, especially when it came to something or someone that she believed belonged to her. Holly's ruined life was a testimony to that. "Then I assume we'll be working with the gardener concerning arrangements."

"The gardener?" Beth gave her a blank look. "Mrs. Winter doesn't employ a gardener."

"But I thought . . ." Chelsea frowned. "What about Jeff? He was pruning the bushes, and I assumed . . ." She couldn't finish; there was a strange weakness in her shoulders.

"Oh, Jeff." Beth laughed. "Jeff loves to garden, but he's not an employee."

"He's not?"

"Far from it. He's Mrs. Winter's son by her first marriage."

Chapter Three

CHELSEA'S FACE WAS ALMOST AS PINK AS her blouse when she headed the van down the long driveway that circled the Winter estate. Beth's stunning revelation had made the color leap instantly into her cheeks; she hadn't been able to come up with any response other than a weak, "Oh, I didn't realize," as she fumbled to regain her composure.

As soon as the van doors were safely shut, Lori let out a low whistle. "Wow! What a faux pas! But I don't blame you, Chels; I thought the same thing. He doesn't *look* anything like his mother."

Chelsea remembered Jeff's hand on her arm as she struggled to muster a small scrap of dignity. "He led me on, Lori. He never corrected me when I referred to Muriel as his employer. He was playing some kind of sick game."

Lori frowned sympathetically. "You didn't say anything incriminating when the two of you were alone, did you?"

"I hope not. But I'm afraid I got a bit carried away on the subject of Queen Muriel. You know me."

"Only too well. Let's just hope he's not one of

those loyal sons who confides everything to his mother."

Chelsea sighed.

"I wonder if there's anything we can do for damage control." Lori stroked the smooth skin of her forehead, as if to erase nonexistent wrinkles. "Do you think there's any way you could convince him you were joking?"

"I don't know." Chelsea suddenly remembered Jeff's suggestion that they spend the afternoon together. "Oh God," she said dismally. "I guess I'll have to go out with him."

"What? He asked you out?"

Chelsea nodded. "While we were waiting for you to get back. I had to mention Stuart to hold him off."

"Ah, the old Stuart ploy again. When are you going to come clean with the rest of the world and admit that he's just a good friend?"

Chelsea shot her a dark look. "He's more than that, and you know it, Lori. We tell each other everything. We're practically soul mates."

"So you say, but I don't see the two of you setting a wedding date anytime soon."

"Marriage isn't the goal of my existence, sis. Besides, our relationship isn't like that. We don't make emotional demands on each other."

"Meaning neither of you is ready to commit yourself. How many great guys have you turned down because of your relationship with Stuart? I would never have met Paul if I'd followed your example."

"You live your life, I'll live mine." Chelsea turned onto Route 1, heading toward Portland. "Do you still want me to drop you at Paul's office?"

"Please." Lori was still looking at her with a sad

expression. "I'm sorry, Chels. And you're right about living your own life. It's just that I love you."

"I know. I love you too."

"So what are you going to do?"

"Call Jeff Blaine, I guess. Tell him I've changed my mind, that I'd like to go out with him. Then find a way to persuade him that I think Mrs. Winter is God's gift to the coast of Maine."

Lori laughed. "That'll take more acting talent than even you possess, Chels."

"What choice do I have? I might as well give it my best shot."

"I wish I could be a fly on the wall when you make that phone call."

"No way, sis. I'm going to have to spend several hours just working up my nerve."

"Chelsea Adams, having to work up nerve? That's got to be a first."

"Don't get nasty." Chelsea checked her rearview mirror. They were coming into Portland and the traffic was heavier. Up ahead she could see smoke-gray buildings against the skyline and the glint of Back Cove in the distance.

"Well, don't wait too long," said Lori. "Or he'll get himself another date. I had the impression that Mr. Blaine and Miss Harmon were pretty interested in each other."

Chelsea glanced over at her. "You noticed it too?"

"It was hard to miss. Not that I'm surprised. He looks like a heartbreaker to me."

"I know what you mean." Chelsea thought of Jeff's dark eyes and felt an unexpected twinge of excitement in the pit of her stomach. "Looks like Mrs. Winter's sons were both cut from the same cloth."

* * *

Chelsea picked up the phone and put it down again three times before she finally dialed. Sitting in the Strawberry Lace kitchen while she waited for a pan of pastry cups to bake, Chelsea had to finally threaten herself with the fact that the future of Strawberry Lace was in jeopardy. Her mouth as dry as if it had just been sand-scoured, she punched the buttons one by one and listened to the buzz that signaled the phone ringing on the other end of the line. What if Jeff picked up the phone himself? What would she say? Or, even worse, what if Muriel Winter answered?

It was picked up on the third ring. "Winter estate. Beth Harmon speaking. May I help you?"

Chelsea felt a wave of relief that dissipated almost instantly. "Beth, this is Chelsea Adams."

"Oh, hi, Chelsea! What can I do for you? Did we forget to cover something?"

"No, everything's fine. I'd like to . . . I was wondering if I could . . ." She stopped, swallowed. "Is Mr. Blaine there?"

"Jeff?" There was a note of surprise in the pleasant voice.

"Yes, I'd like to speak to him."

"Just a moment, please." There was a click, then the dead tone that told her she'd been put on hold. She hated that; she always felt as if she were in a box or something, with the cover nailed on. Unable to hear the sound of approaching footsteps or voices in the background, she didn't know when the phone would be picked up. She closed her eyes, twisted a curl of hair around her finger, counted mentally to ten. Once, twice, three times.

"Hello, Chelsea." It was Jeff's voice, but she couldn't read it. Was he pleased she had called? Or irritated at being interrupted? There was no clue in his tone. "What can I do for you?"

She sucked air into her lungs. "I wanted to let you know—" She stopped. She couldn't believe she was actually calling up a guy and telling him she'd changed her mind. She wasn't the kind of person who changed her mind about things; once she'd decided something, she always stuck to her guns.

"Is something wrong?" His voice sounded a little warmer, which gave her courage to continue.

"No, it's about that invitation to go to the beach this afternoon."

"Yes?"

He obviously wasn't going to make this easy for her. Maybe he was angry about her rejection. Some men, she knew, were extremely sensitive about such things, although he certainly hadn't struck her as that type at all. More the opposite. She had a reckless impulse to hang up.

Well, she couldn't. She didn't have a choice. She had to make some connection with him, had to be sure that he wouldn't repeat her comments to his mother. It had to be done for the sake of the business. She glanced over her shoulder at the shining row of cake pans she'd lined up on the big central worktable for the afternoon's baking. They were catering a fortieth birthday party tomorrow afternoon. She'd have to reschedule the baking for tonight.

"My afternoon's freer than I realized. I hope it's not too late to accept."

There was a short silence. She almost died, waiting for his answer. Please, dear God, make him say yes, she prayed. Make everything be all right.

Finally his voice came to her. "I thought you said you were involved with someone."

She could have kicked herself for not thinking her way out of this impasse ahead of time. She looked helplessly at the ceiling as if there might be some answer written there. Nothing.

"Well," she said, groping for inspiration, "it's kind of an off-again, on-again thing."

"Oh. And right now it's off?"

"Sort of."

"You've had a fight."

"Not exactly." She might as well just plunge in and make up some wild story; she couldn't get in any deeper than she already was. "We've decided to give each other some space. See other people for a while."

"Sounds like he's got his eye on another woman."

"I don't know. Maybe." She couldn't believe she was talking this way, casually lying about her relationship with Stuart. And, on top of that, practically begging this breathtakingly handsome man to go out with her. It wasn't the kind of thing she'd ever done, nothing she'd do in a million years. "So, anyway, is the invitation still open? Can we go to the beach?"

"Sure."

She wished he sounded a little more enthusiastic. Maybe he didn't believe her; maybe he thought she was playing with him. Which, in a way, she was. But only for the sake of the business, she reminded herself sharply. Otherwise, she'd be up to her elbows in cake batter right now.

"Good," she said. "Where should I meet you?"

"I'll pick you up."

"Fine. My apartment's right over the Strawberry Lace shop, opposite—"

"I know where it is," he said abruptly. "I'll be there in thirty minutes."

In her bedroom, Chelsea pulled on her old black bathing suit, wishing she'd splurged and bought a new one two weeks ago, when Lori suggested it. At the time, it hadn't seemed important. Stuart didn't care what she wore; she was used to swimming with him in cutoffs and a tank top when they went to the beach. Which wasn't often. Neither of them were eager swimmers; growing up so close to the ocean built a certain respect into a person; you learned early that the sea wasn't something to fool around with. Besides, both she and Stuart preferred spending their free time on *Chelsea's Choice*.

She hoped she hadn't made a big mistake, taking the afternoon off. She'd have to spend the whole evening baking now, not her favorite activity when she was tired. But it couldn't be helped. She had to mend her fences, and mend them well.

She stuffed her beach towel, blue terry cover-up, and a large bottle of sunscreen into her canvas tote bag, then slipped into a pair of pink cotton shorts and a matching cotton knit shirt. She had to make the most of her assets on this crucial afternoon, and pink brought out the rose tones in her skin and set off her hair. In the bathroom she freshened her makeup, twisted her hair into a loose knot at the top of her head, and slipped gold hoops into her ears, before admiring the effect in the mirror. She smiled and gave herself a thumbs-up. If this look didn't affect Jeff Blaine, then she'd eat her towel.

She grabbed her woven sea-grass hat and pushed it down onto her head just as the doorbell rang, so she didn't have time to check herself again in the mirror. But she remembered how the lacy shadows had played across her face one hot afternoon last summer aboard the *Chelsea,* creating an effect so charming that Stuart had remarked about it for days.

The doorbell rang again. She took a deep breath and opened the door.

"Hi, Jeff! Come on in." She made her voice bright and cheery. "Would you like something to drink before we leave?"

Jeff didn't move, just stood looking down at her with those incredible eyes. They briefly swept over her body and then returned to her face before he answered. "No thanks. I think we'd better get going."

"Sure. I'm all set." She slid her tote bag onto her arm. She felt a little more nervous than she'd expected. Was it because he wasn't smiling?

"I was thinking we'd go out to Hillcrest Beach, if that's okay with you."

"Fine. I'm almost ashamed to admit I haven't been there since I was a kid."

"It's gorgeous," he said. "The surf's spectacular. By the way, you look great."

"Thanks. So do you."

He really did look good. Like he'd just stepped out of an L.L. Bean catalogue. He was wearing white shorts and a blue knit shirt. His feet were settled comfortably into a worn pair of Birkenstock sandals.

She locked the door and led him down the narrow wooden stairs to the apartment entrance. She'd been thrilled, three years ago, to buy this place at a bargain price. It was the perfect setup: the downstairs shop with its large display window where she and Lori created sophisticated arrangements enchanting enough to attract customers in off the street; the small reception room, decorated in pink and white, with its easy chairs and stacks of picture albums featuring the most elegant affairs catered by Strawberry Lace; the huge kitchen behind, with its wide counters and shining appliances, the pots and pans suspended attractively and conveniently from long beams above the counters. And upstairs the perfect two-bedroom apartment, which had only needed a little attention to give it a homelike feel.

When she stepped out onto the sidewalk, Chelsea's eyes went directly to the rusted gray Chevy Nova parked in front of the shop. For a minute she thought it might belong to a customer at the beauty shop next door, then Jeff took a set of keys out of his pocket and unlocked the passenger door.

"This is your car?" She felt a twinge of disappointment. She'd expected something with a little class: a Jaguar, maybe, or a BMW.

He opened the door. "Yeah, this is Old Faithful. I've had her since college." He patted the roof. "Wouldn't part with her for love or money."

She slid into the passenger seat and watched him circle the car to get in on the driver's side. He pushed the key into the ignition and started the engine, which rattled a loud complaint, before he pulled out into the street.

"I have to admit, I was surprised to hear from you," he said. "I thought you were giving me the brush-off this morning."

Chelsea tried a light laugh, but it came out as more of a whine. She was distinctly uncomfortable, growing more so by the minute. Jeff had yet to even smile at her. She wondered, with a little tickle of fear, if he was the kind of man who punished women who rebuffed him. She'd heard of men like that, psychopathic types who took all their frustrations out on females.

"I guess the idea of going to the beach sounded better and better to me the more I thought about it," she said carefully. "I hope you weren't offended by my behavior at the house."

He shook his head. "Not offended. Intrigued. I can't quite figure you out."

"Well, that's not too surprising. We only met a couple of hours ago."

"I'm pretty good at judging people. My first impressions are nearly always right."

She tried another laugh. "So I guess I'm supposed to ask what your first impression was."

"I didn't say I *revealed* my first impression." Finally, she caught the ghost of a smile. "That would be irresponsible. 'What we have to do is be forever curiously testing new opinions and courting new impressions.' "

"That sounds like a quote."

"It is. Walter Pater."

"You memorize that kind of stuff?"

"I'm afraid reading poetry and philosophy is one of my weaknesses. It's an addiction. I really can't help myself." He glanced at her again and his smile broadened.

Chelsea smiled back at him. He was starting to loosen up. Now she just had to figure out a way to bring up the subject of Muriel Winter again so she could convince him that she'd been joking that morning. She studied the chiseled line of his jaw as he watched the road ahead. He didn't look anything like Brandon, who was shorter and less muscular, with thick blond hair. Their personalities weren't alike either. Brandon was outgoing and hearty, with the kind of carefree attitude that made him easy to talk to. Jeff was friendly enough, but there was something mysterious about him, a hint of remoteness that made her think he might be hiding a secret. You'd never guess they were brothers. Half brothers, she corrected herself.

"So what's your passion?" Jeff asked, jolting her out of her thoughts. "What do you do in your free time?"

"Free time? I don't usually have any to spare." She thought suddenly of *Chelsea's Choice*. "Actually, my favorite thing is to spend a whole day out on the water."

He slowed to turn left. "You sail." It was a statement, not a question.

"No. I usually go out in my friend's lobster boat. I'm ashamed to admit it, but I've never actually set foot on a sailboat."

She half expected him to make some comment on this deprivation, or at least to invite her out on the family yacht, but he didn't say anything. Then she remembered, with a little ripple of resentment, that he still thought she believed he was the gardener. Apparently he was content to keep up the pretense, and he wasn't going to tell her his real identity. Maybe he liked slumming. He obviously had a little thing going with Beth Harmon. She wondered if his mother knew about his habits. Her mouth shaped itself into a wry smile. Muriel would undoubtedly have a fit if she knew he was involved with an employee.

She could see the brown and white beach entrance sign up ahead. Jeff slowed the car, which gave a couple of loud clanks from deep within its engine as he stopped in front of the ticket booth. He pulled a five-dollar bill out of his shorts pocket and handed it to the attendant, who gave him a pair of orange tickets.

"Have a nice day," said the attendant.

"You bet." He put the car into gear and headed down a narrow asphalt road to the parking lot. In front of them a ridge of high sand dunes blocked their view of the water.

"I really appreciate this invitation," Chelsea said, after he parked and they got out. "It's a great beach day. For May, at least."

"My thoughts precisely." Jeff grinned at her over the top of the car. "I'm glad you changed your mind."

Chelsea felt her cheeks go warm. She leaned into the car and retrieved her tote bag while Jeff went around and unlocked the trunk. He lifted out a small cooler and a folded green plaid blanket. "Oh," he said suddenly, "I almost forgot." He straightened and fixed her with a solemn look. "I have a message for you from Mrs. Winter."

Chapter Four

MESSAGE?" CHELSEA STRUGGLED TO KEEP her voice cool. "I hope nothing's wrong."

He shrugged and closed the trunk. "She wants to talk with you. Tomorrow morning at ten. Privately."

Something *was* wrong. Muriel Winter wasn't the type to request private interviews with the help unless there were problems. Jeff had obviously told his mother about her comments and she intended to cancel the arrangements; another catering service would be hired for the Independence Day party. Chelsea felt a rush of anger. Why hadn't he said something earlier? Why drive all the way out to the beach before he dropped his bomb? She tightened her grip on her tote bag.

"Do you know what she wants to talk about?"

"How would I know? I'm just the gardener."

She saw the glint in his dark eyes, the quirk of his mouth, and knew he was playing with her, that he'd go on playing with her all afternoon unless she said something. It was the most distinctly uncomfortable feeling she'd had in months.

She took a deep breath. She should just tell him

that she knew who he was and take the consequences. Maybe he'd be moved by her honesty.

"Jeff . . ." She stepped toward him and found herself startlingly close as he moved in her direction simultaneously. She placed her free hand on the car to steady herself.

"Don't you think we'd better go find a good spot on the beach?" He brushed past her and headed up a gravel walkway toward the dunes. He walked fast, his muscular legs taking him quickly up the slope. She stared after him for a minute. Had he guessed what she was going to say? Had he deliberately avoided hearing her confession? She ran to catch up with him, but didn't reach him until she'd climbed to the top of the steep dune.

"Look at those breakers." He pointed down the dune toward the long, gray beach and the ocean beyond. "Do you bodysurf?"

She shook her head and tried again to catch her breath, but before she could speak, he was jogging down the side of the dune. Chelsea followed, grateful for the hat that shielded her eyes from the sharp glare of sunlight on the water. Rolling toward them in tall, whitecapped waves, the ocean stretched to the horizon. Straight ahead and connected to the beach by a narrow sandbar was a small island, rising out of the water like the brown and green back of an enormous sea creature. The beach stretched in both directions as far as she could see. It was largely empty; only a few people were there, spread out on blankets and towels. A couple of children were building a sand castle at the water's edge. A blue and white beach umbrella shielded a small mesh playpen holding a sleeping child. In the distance to her right, two men threw a football back and forth.

Jeff had already spread out the blanket and was stripping off his shirt when she reached him. He handed her a bottle of sun-block lotion. "Would you mind doing my back?"

"Sure." Chelsea squirted the thick white lotion into her palm and started spreading it on the muscular back Jeff presented. As her hand slid over his tanned skin, an odd little jolt of electricity ran through her fingers and up her arm to her shoulder.

Stop that, she told herself. The weird excitement she felt didn't make any sense. Hadn't she spread sun block on Stuart's back a thousand times? And wasn't this man someone she clearly didn't like? The kind of man who would let her go on believing a lie, who would exploit her ignorance for all it was worth? He was Muriel Winter's son, all right; that was as clear as day.

"There. All done." She pushed away the peculiar yearning and handed him back the bottle.

"Thanks. Now it's your turn." He was smiling down at her again.

He looks like a Greek god, she thought reflexively, and then pushed that thought away too. She shook her head. "It's not necessary. I'm fine."

"Are you kidding? Your skin is so fair it's almost translucent. Come on, take off your shirt." When she didn't move, he reached out and tugged her shirttail out of her shorts.

"Hey!" She twisted away from him. "I can take off my own shirt, thank you very much."

"Good. Then do it. I want to get this stuff on you before you start blistering right before my eyes."

Acutely aware of his scrutiny, she skimmed off her shirt and slipped quickly out of her shorts, then turned her back to him. A moment later she felt his hands on her shoulders, cool and slippery, caressing her arms and back. He worked slowly, as if savoring the texture of her skin. She felt hot, electric shivers at the nape of her neck. Her back tingled under his hands. The sensation of heat increased, spread down her spine, through her whole body. She realized with a jolt of surprise that she was becoming sexually aroused.

She stepped quickly away from him. "Thanks." She opened her tote bag to hide her acute consternation.

"But I'm not finished." He was holding the bottle, smiling at her with those dark, wicked eyes and that incredible dimple.

"That's okay." She fished out her towel and wrapped it around her. Her whole body was on fire.

He capped the bottle and dropped it onto the blanket. His mouth looked like it was having a hard time holding in a laugh. He glanced over his shoulder at the water and rubbed his hands together. "How about a bodysurfing lesson?"

"You're kidding. It's only the third week in May. The water's freezing!"

He raised one dark eyebrow. "I thought you were a native Mainer."

"I am, but that doesn't mean I'm demented."

He laughed. "Come on. It's not bad once you get in."

"No thanks. You go ahead. I'll catch a few rays." She sat down on the blanket.

"Okay. But you don't know what you're missing." And then he was running down the sand to the water. Chelsea watched him, measuring his athletic stride with her eyes. She could tell that he was powerful; he was probably one of those rich men who took expensive vitamins and worked out at a health club every day. You didn't get a body like that without a lot of investment. Why did she have such a strong reaction to his touch, though? Why did his dark eyes disturb her so deeply? She lay down on the blanket abruptly, so she wouldn't have to see his muscular sprint into the surf.

He came back, drenched and exhilarated, his taut body raining drops down on the blanket, his hair lying in dark strands across his forehead. He toweled off, standing over her, his legs braced apart in the warm sand.

"I think you'd better let me finish putting sun block on you, Chelsea. You've already got a red stripe across your lower back."

"Do I? Oh, damn!" Chelsea reached for the bottle of sun block, but he was already pouring some into his hand. "Lie back down," he commanded.

She did as he said, and felt his hand on the small of her back, stroking slowly and smoothly toward her buttocks. The same erotic sensation overwhelmed her, and it was all she could do not to moan.

"Want me to do your legs too? They look a little fiery."

"No thanks. I can do them myself." She sat up and took the bottle from him, squirted lotion quickly into her palm and massaged the backs of her thighs and calves. He watched her for a minute and then stretched out beside her on the blanket. "Just let me know when you want that bodysurfing lesson." He closed his eyes.

She found herself staring down at him, admiring his pectoral muscles and the rugged contour of his jaw. He was utterly handsome, the kind of man most women would die for. She wished that Judy Pierce, her old high school nemesis, would come walking by and see her now. She'd probably say something snotty like, "Oh, I didn't recognize you, Chels. You've lost so much weight." And then she'd start flirting with Jeff. But the next morning the news would be all over town that Chelsea Adams had finally snared herself a very sexy man.

She reminded herself sharply that she wasn't interested in a relationship with Jeff Blaine. The whole reason she was here, the reason she'd come to the beach with him in the first place, was to straighten things out before they got more complicated than they already were. She had to convince him that she really had nothing at all against his mother, even if her best friend *had* been engaged to Brandon.

She took a deep breath and stared out to sea, trying to collect her thoughts. She couldn't just blurt everything right out. People in Jeff's world were very smooth and careful in how they presented things. She'd have to engage him in conversation first, talk about something neutral like gardening or some detail of her job. Then lead him gradually into a discussion of the events of that morning. She shifted on her hips to face him.

"Jeff? I was wondering about the best way to prune rosebushes."

He didn't move, didn't even open his eyes to look at her. She watched the slow rise and fall of his chest. It occurred to her that he was sleeping.

"Jeff?" She touched his arm, very lightly, near the elbow.

He didn't respond.

She sighed. He *was* asleep. So much for her wonderful plans. She'd have to put them on hold until he woke up. She glanced down the beach, where the rollers were washing up on the sand. Her body was warm from the sun; it would feel good to cool her feet in the surf. She noted that people were walking along the sandbar out to the island. She got to her feet, found her terry cover-up in her duffel bag, slipped it on and started down the beach.

It was enjoyable to walk; moving seemed to clear her head. She headed out to the island, relishing the coolness of the damp sand on her bare feet. The tide had made little eddies in the sand, so that in places it was packed into hard ridges, like the rib cage of some huge skeleton. She watched a woman point out the phenomenon to her young child. The small, red-haired boy, in bright blue bathing trunks that sagged to his knees, squatted at her feet and poked his finger repeatedly into the ridges. Another child was scrambling up and down a large rock that was partially submerged in the gray sand. Chelsea bent and picked up a long rope of brown seaweed. It was loaded with periwinkles. The tiny snail-like creatures were clinging to the underside of the slick, rubbery leaves. She dropped it at the water's edge, watched a tongue of surf lick it back into the ocean. A light gust of wind caught her hair and spun it across her face. She laughed, pushed it behind her ears and jogged lightly across the rest of the sandbar to the island.

She'd been to this beach only once before, as a child, when both her parents were still alive. She and Lori had begged to go out to the island, and their father had taken them while their mother sunbathed on the beach. They had skipped and danced all the way out, but when it came time to go back over the sandbar, both girls had claimed their legs were too tired. So their father had given them each piggy back rides, alternating the girls on his broad shoulders all the way back to their blanket.

Chelsea smiled fondly at the memory. Her father had been such a strong man, the rock of the world to his daughters' young eyes. Who could have guessed that he would die of a heart attack in his thirty-seventh year? His death had shattered their lives, yet when the girls turned to their distraught mother for comfort, she had nothing to offer. She had neither the strength nor the resilience of their father. All she would talk about was how she needed a man, how a woman had to be in love to be alive. Her grief left her weak, vulnerable to impulse. When she told them, only six months later, that she'd fallen in love and was going to be married, both girls were more relieved than anything else.

Chelsea reached the island and started up the rocky path to the top. She watched her step; it was early in the season and her feet were still too tender to challenge barnacles and sharp stones, not to mention the bits of broken glass and inevitable litter of tourists.

At the top of the island she gazed out at the open sea. There were a few sailboats plying the dark blue water, and farther out, a trawler. She wondered if Stuart was still out on the water; probably he was finished hauling for the day, unless he'd had better luck than usual. She wished she were spending the afternoon with him, rather than trying to figure out how to placate the Winter family for her faux pas. She picked her way down the far side of the island, toward a depression she'd spotted in the rock. It looked like a perfect place to rest, out of the direct path of the wind, but in the comforting sun.

Chelsea settled into the rock basin, which was almost like a cup of granite and noted with pleasure that the rock had been sun-warmed to a pleasant temperature. The sound of surf lapping the granite rocks below her was like a lullaby. She closed her eyes and lay back, stretched out her legs. It was the last thing she knew until a sudden torrent of water drenched her.

Chelsea yelled and jumped to her feet. Even before her sight had cleared from the bleary vision of sleep, she knew what had happened. The tide had come in while she slept, and a huge wave had broken over the rock where she lay. She scrambled to the top of the island, away from the precarious spot. What she saw as she looked back toward the mainland beach jolted her. She gasped, a sharp intake of cold salt air. The sandbar was covered with water. And the tide was still coming in.

She ran down the rocky hillside, ignoring the jagged outcroppings of granite under her bare feet. At the water's edge she hesitated. The beach's expanse was radically diminished and the sand itself was deserted. She must have slept for well over two hours. The spot where Jeff had laid out their blanket was now underwater. Where was Jeff? There was no sign of him, or anyone else, except for a small group of people walking along the dunes in the far distance.

She felt the first jostle of fear, a tiny gnawing sensation in the small of her back. She took a deep breath to calm herself and studied the water in front of her, trying to gauge its depth. It roiled and eddied, splashing up little whitecaps. The chances were, it wasn't very deep. Probably she'd be able to wade across. At its deepest, the sea would likely only come up to her calves.

She stepped tentatively into the water. It swirled over her feet and around her ankles. It was numbingly cold, but that was to be expected this time of the year. The water off the Maine coast was never tepid, even in the hottest days of summer. She took another deep breath and started walking, driving through the water with a long, powerful stride. It splashed over her feet and up against her legs, but it wasn't deep. She fixed her gaze on the shore, three hundred yards away. She'd make it easily. She had to.

It wasn't until she was in the middle of the submerged sandbar, halfway between the island and the beach, that she felt the undertow. She was up to her knees in freezing water, and the first surge caught her unprepared. It came from behind, a sudden, hard shove, like a huge bar of steel sweeping through the water. She stumbled, swayed, and just managed to recover her balance. She continued walking, more slowly, carefully planting each foot in the sand, bracing her legs for stability.

The second surge hit even harder. She staggered, fell, caught herself with her hands and scrambled quickly to her feet. She knew—growing up on the coast, she'd been told a thousand times—that panic was her worst enemy. The ocean wasn't something you could fight. You had to work with it to survive. But all her training, all her years of knowledge, disappeared in the sudden flash of heat in her brain. Panic seized her, shredded her ability to think, drove her frantically toward the shore. She had only one thought: to get to the beach. She started running.

Immediately, another rip attacked her, pushing

her sideways. This time her legs went out from under her and she struggled desperately to find purchase in the sand underfoot. But it seemed to have disappeared, as if, in that one rush of water, the whole sandbar had been torn out from under her and driven into the sea. She opened her mouth to scream, and water swirled into it. She choked, coughed, spit, gulped for air. Her arms and legs thrashed wildly, fighting to keep her afloat, to find something to hang onto. A wave broke over her head. She was pressed down rapidly into the swirling, green tide. Something flashed behind her eyes and she was flung backward. A bright pain blossomed on the side of her head. She flailed again and emerged suddenly into air, gasping. Her vision blurred; she shook her head to focus, her arms and legs still beating the water frantically.

But what she saw, when her sight finally cleared, made her chest clench and her legs lock into long, useless poles. The riptide was pulling her back toward the island, straight into a jagged wall of granite. Within seconds she would be smashed against the rocks by the relentless power of the undertow.

Chapter Five

CHELSEA SAW THE DOUGHNUT-SHAPED life preserver sail through the air and land a few feet from her. But it lay there rocking for a full minute before she came to herself enough to realize what it was. She struggled toward it, kicking with her numb legs, reaching desperately with her frozen hands. Finally, she managed to grab it. Only then did she turn clumsily to see where it had come from.

Jeff Blaine, all six feet of him, was standing in the bow of a small skiff, shouting orders.

She gaped at him, her mind blank.

"Hang on!" he shouted. "I'm pulling you in!"

She clutched the life preserver and felt herself moving rapidly over the top of the water. Moments later she was being hauled aboard the boat, Jeff's powerful arms enveloping her rib cage, his legs braced in the rocking boat for balance. She coughed and shivered, pressed the whole length of her body against him just for warmth and the desperate need to touch something solid.

He wrapped her in a blanket which she vaguely recognized as the one he'd spread earlier on the sand. She knew he was talking to her, but her brain was still numb, her head throbbing with pain, and she couldn't make out what he was saying. He pushed her down into the bottom of the boat, turning her on her side so she could cough out the remaining seawater in her frozen lungs. He bent over her, frowning, examining her head where the pain was centered, probing her scalp with his fingers. When she winced and cried out, he drew his hand away. She was stunned to see that his fingers were stained with blood.

He scrambled into the stern and turned his attention to the outboard motor there, steering quickly away from the treacherous riptide. A moment later Chelsea started shivering. Her teeth chattered violently; her body rocked in spasms. She watched Jeff in a kind of dazed stupor.

He kept one eye on her and one on the water ahead. But it wasn't until they had rounded the island that he spoke. "Looks like you hit a rock when you went under. Are you dizzy?"

"A little." She reached to feel the throbbing lump on her head and winced sharply.

"Don't touch it!" he commanded. "And don't close your eyes. Keep them focused on me. You're going to be all right, but it was a close call. It's a good thing I figured out where you were and had the sense to go after a boat when I did."

She spoke around her chattering teeth. "Thank you. I was so . . . so . . . scared."

He nodded perfunctorily. "I'm taking you to the hospital."

"No!" She coughed and tried to sit up. "You don't need to. I'm fine."

He pushed her back down. "You've just experienced major head trauma. And you may be suffering from shock. You need to be examined."

"No." Numb as her brain was, she knew she had to prevent him from taking her to the hospital. "I can't go to the hospital."

"Of course you can. You have to."

"No. Really. I can't."

"Why not?"

She looked away from him. How could she tell him, this man who probably had millions at his disposal, that she had no medical insurance? That she couldn't afford even emergency room service? Strawberry Lace was a shoestring business, a hand-to-mouth operation. Someday, she and Lori had promised each other, they'd have enough to buy health insurance. But that day hadn't arrived.

"Have you had a bad experience in a hospital or something?" He was watching her curiously, waiting for an answer.

"Not exactly. It's something I'd rather not talk about." She tried to smile. Her mouth felt stiff from cold. "Please, I'm fine. Honestly. Can't we just leave it at that?"

"I'm afraid not."

"You're going to have to. I'm not going to a hospital. Or anyplace else but home. I told you, I'm fine."

"You're a pretty stubborn woman, aren't you?"

"I've been called worse." She glanced back at the island and the water roiling over the sandbar. "I prefer to say I'm determined."

He laughed. "All right, Chelsea, I'll forgo the hospital, as long as you let me fix you some hot soup and tuck you into a nice warm bed after I take you home."

She shivered again and hugged the blanket closer around her. "It's a deal."

She hadn't realized it would be quite so unsettling, having Jeff Blaine in her apartment. He took charge the minute she unlocked the door, holding her by the elbow and steering her through the living room and into her bedroom as if he knew the layout of the place.

He flicked on the overhead light. "I want to take a good look at that wound."

"Ouch!" she cried as his fingers explored her injured scalp.

He finally released her. "I think it'll be okay. Make sure you wash it gently and thoroughly."

"Of course! What kind of an idiot do you think I am?"

He ignored her indignant glare. "You get out of that wet suit and take a hot shower. Then we'll have dinner."

Before she could protest, he had left the room, closing the door behind him. She sighed and slumped onto her bed. She knew he was right. All she wanted was to get warm and dry. She shrugged off the blanket, stripped off her bathing suit and glanced briefly in the long mirror on her closet door. Her skin was peppered with goose bumps and her lips had a dark blue cast. Her hair hung in damp, clotted ropes over her shoulders. One of the strands was stained with blood. Her makeup had washed off and her nose had reddened unattractively in the cold water. She looked like a half-drowned cat.

She wondered what Jeff Blaine thought of her now. He was probably thoroughly disgusted. Apparently he'd decided to cloak his feelings so that he could continue stringing her along, letting her believe he was Muriel Winter's gardener. She opened her closet and took out her bathrobe. It had belonged to her father and was the only one she had, a blue terry-cloth one, worn through at the elbows. She wished now that she'd splurged the last time she was at the mall and bought herself that teal-blue velour robe she'd had her eye on. It was one of her best colors; it brought out the green tint in her eyes and heightened the natural pink of her cheeks. But it had been expensive—almost seventy dollars—and seemed an unnecessary luxury at the time.

She sighed, slipped into the robe and opened the bedroom door. She was relieved to hear the rattle of pots; Jeff was in the kitchen. She could sneak through the living room to the bathroom while he was busy.

She was almost to the bathroom door when she heard his chuckle. She turned to find him standing in the kitchen doorway, his hands braced lazily on the frame, grinning at her.

"Where'd you get that thing?" He nodded at her robe. "It looks like it belonged to your grandfather."

She didn't reward him with a reply, just went into the bathroom and slammed the door.

"Hey, take it easy. I didn't mean anything by that."

She clamped her mouth shut and took off the robe, hung it on the hook on the back of the door. She saw that Jeff had already filled the tub with water. She leaned down and tested it with her wrist. Nice and hot; just the way she liked it.

Then she heard him laugh again and realized he was still standing outside the door. "*Is* it your grandfather's?"

"No!" If the door hadn't been between them, she'd have picked up the air freshener bottle and thrown it at him. "Do you mind if I take my bath in peace?"

"Sorry. Just teasing. One of my many failings, I'm afraid. I'll go finish dinner." She heard his footsteps moving away from the door, but it took her several minutes before she could relax enough to lower herself into the hot tub.

An hour later, Chelsea was sitting across from Jeff at her kitchen table, dipping her spoon into a bowl of vegetable soup and inhaling the mouth-watering aroma of fresh-baked bran muffins. She was wearing her jeans and her green fleece shirt. In spite of her bath, she still felt chilled.

"Where did you get the muffin recipe?" she asked, her eyes wide with astonishment after she took her first bite.

"Family secret."

"It's delicious!" She took another bite. Was it because she was so hungry, or because she'd almost drowned? Everything tasted fantastic. She had to get the recipe out of him somehow. "Could I persuade you to share it?"

"Afraid not. It's my mother's recipe. She makes them every Sunday morning."

Chelsea almost choked. "Your *mother?*" She couldn't imagine Muriel Winter lifting a finger in the kitchen, let alone mixing up these delectable muffins.

"Yes, my mother. What's so strange about that?"

Now it was her turn to grin. "It's just that . . ." She shook her head. "I'm sorry, I just can't imagine your mother cooking anything."

His eyes narrowed and she realized she'd blown it. So much for letting him believe she thought he was the gardener. She wanted to kick herself. After all her careful plans about how to make Jeff think she admired Muriel Winter, she'd gone and run off at the mouth. She could almost hear Lori chastising her.

"Why can't you imagine my mother cooking? What do you know about my mother?"

She put down her muffin, placed both hands on the table. She tried not to smile. "All right, I have to confess I know who you are. Beth told me."

"Oh? And what did she tell you?"

"That you're not the gardener. You're Muriel Winter's son."

"What does that have to do with my mother?" He leaned back in his chair and laced his arms across his chest. She couldn't read his face, didn't know if he was angry or amused.

"Nothing, except that I can't imagine Muriel Winter baking muffins. Ever." She grinned again. Just the thought made her want to laugh out loud.

"Why not?"

"Well, she's just . . . she's so . . ." Chelsea slid her hands off the table, dropped them into her lap. "She doesn't seem like the type, that's all."

"Exactly what type do you think she is?"

"I didn't mean to offend you. It's just that she strikes me as the kind of person who wouldn't . . ." She groped for words, for some way to phrase her thoughts delicately. "Well, you know, someone who's so . . ."

"So rich she wouldn't get her hands dirty, is that it?"

She flushed. "I wasn't going to put it that way."

"But that's what you meant, isn't it?" He pushed his chair back.

"Look, I'm sorry. Honestly." She tried to soften his glare with a smile, but his expression didn't change. "I like your mother. She's a very . . ." She searched for a word. ". . . an elegant woman, with a lot of class."

"Didn't you tell me earlier that she caused your friend's broken heart?"

"Yes, but that was ages ago, and anyway, it was Brandon—"

"My brother." He nodded. His jaw looked very hard. "Why don't you just be honest, Chelsea? You don't like my mother at all. You as much as told me so, back at the house."

"That isn't what I said!" Her alarm turned to anger. "Anyway, I didn't know who you were. I thought you were the gardener!"

"So you said."

"And you didn't correct me! You let me go on believing you were an employee! You let—no, you *encouraged*—me to make a fool of myself!"

"You didn't need any help."

She shoved her chair violently away from the table and stood up. "I think you'd better leave."

He got to his feet. "That's a good idea." He gave her one last, blazing scowl, turned on his heel and headed for the door.

He was reaching for the doorknob when panic flooded her. She ran after him. "You're not going to tell her what I said, are you?"

He turned and regarded her coldly.

"Please, Jeff, give me a break. I really need this job." She felt horrible. She'd never begged anybody for anything in her life. Yet now she was begging this man, and all because she hadn't been able to control her big mouth.

"I'll think about it." He wasn't going to give her any promises, that was obvious. She'd just have to hope that he would keep his mouth shut.

She let her arms drop limply to her sides as he opened the door. "Thanks for saving me," she said despondently.

He glanced back over his shoulder. "It was my pleasure." His expression was unreadable; she didn't know if he was mocking her or if there was a grain of sincerity behind his words. "Don't forget the meeting with my mother. Ten o'clock sharp."

Then he was gone, hurrying down the narrow wooden stairs to the street without a backward look.

Chelsea stood staring after him. She felt dizzy and sick to her stomach. It was a long time before she turned and went back into her apartment.

Chelsea knew she'd have to tell Lori; she couldn't sweep something like this under the rug. Chances were that Muriel Winter's ten o'clock meeting would be a painful reprimand and a summary cancellation of the contract. She'd have to prepare her sister for what was coming.

But it was Stuart she called first, spending over an hour spilling her tale of woe into his patient silence, knowing that, of all her friends and family, only Stuart could really understand the agony she'd been through.

He was earnestly sympathetic. "Sounds like you've earned a trip out to Eagle Island. How about tomorrow after I'm done hauling?"

"I'd love to, but I have that college graduation party. Could we do it Thursday instead?"

"Sure can." His tone changed to concern. "I don't like the sound of your head injury, Chels. Maybe you shouldn't be alone tonight. Want me to come over?"

"Thanks, but I've got hours of baking ahead of me, and you'd only be in the way. No offense."

He laughed. "Don't worry. I know how you get when you're cooking. It's safer if I keep my distance. But listen, call me tomorrow and let me know how you are."

"Of course. When was the last day we didn't talk to each other at least once?"

She felt better after her conversation with Stuart, but she knew she'd still have to call Lori, or her conscience would bother her all night. After she'd mixed up the cake batter, poured it into the big baking sheets, and slid them into the ovens, she worked up the courage to pick up the phone.

She made light of her adventure at the beach, and concentrated on the problem of Muriel. Lori sounded disappointed but typically optimistic. "You don't know for sure that's what she's going to say. Maybe Jeff didn't tell her anything."

"If he didn't before, he probably has by now. I got in an argument with him before he left."

"Oh God. Chelsea, how could you?"

"I don't know. I wasn't thinking. Maybe I was still in shock from my narrow escape. What can I say? I'm sorry, sis."

Lori sighed. "Well, it's water under the bridge at this point. I'm glad you're safe and sound. Would you like me to come with you tomorrow morning for moral support?"

"I don't know. Jeff said something about Muriel wanting to talk to me privately. If she *is* going to bawl me out, I guess I'd rather there weren't any witnesses."

Lori murmured her agreement. "You want some help with the petits fours tonight? I could come over for about an hour."

"No thanks, I've got everything under control. Say hi to Paul for me."

"Will do."

Chelsea hung up slowly. The sad, empty feeling inside her chest wouldn't go away. She looked around at the big shop kitchen. She'd spent so many hours here, creating culinary works of art. She loved Strawberry Lace and everything about it. She couldn't bear the thought of going out of business. Especially because of her own stupidity.

She wiped away a tear and straightened her shoulders. There wasn't any point in moping around. She had to do what she had to do, and tonight that meant creating 112 petits fours for tomorrow's college graduation party at the Cumberland Country Club.

It was almost nine when Chelsea woke the next morning. She took one look at the clock, gasped and stumbled out of bed to the bathroom, her eyes still blurry with sleep. In the shower, she tried to make herself wake up, but the more awake she became, the more tension gripped her at the thought of what lay ahead. She had hoped that a good night's sleep would refresh her enough to help her envision the interview with Muriel Winter in a positive light. But it hadn't worked; it hadn't even been a good night's sleep. She'd tossed and turned, pestered by dreams of water and wild roses and long sand beaches, along which Jeff Blaine strolled with a look of serene composure.

She skipped breakfast, dressed in her tailored beige suit and her pearls, then discarded it for the safety of her signature Strawberry Lace outfit. By nine-thirty she was headed up Route 1, mentally rehearsing the coming events of the day. The plans were to meet Lori at the country club at noon, where they would do the on-site preparations. The party was scheduled for seven.

She arrived at the Winter estate just a few minutes before ten, and took the van dutifully around to the service entrance. She prayed, as she walked across the courtyard to the door, that it wouldn't be Jeff who answered her ring this time. She wasn't up to facing him this morning.

She was relieved when Beth opened the door. "Hi, Chelsea! What can I do for you?"

"I have a ten o'clock appointment with Mrs. Winter."

She frowned. "Are you sure?"

"That's what I was told."

"That's odd. Nothing was said to me. Well, come on in." Beth ushered Chelsea into the entryway and asked her to wait, then disappeared through a paneled door. When she returned, several minutes later, she looked troubled.

"Mrs. Winter is busy at the moment, but you could wait for her if you like."

"It was Mrs. Winter who scheduled the appointment. I assumed that she'd be waiting for me."

Beth smiled wanly. "Why don't you wait in the library?" She led Chelsea up the stairs, down a long hall, and into a darkpaneled room.

"How long will she be?" Chelsea tried to keep the

frustration out of her voice. She was angry, growing more furious by the minute, at the way she was being treated, no doubt at Muriel's orders.

"I'm sorry. I have no idea. Please, make yourself comfortable." Beth nodded briefly toward one of the leather easy chairs and withdrew, closing the door behind her. Chelsea glanced at the elegant antique vase that decorated the central table. She had half a mind to pick it up and smash it against the floor. Or maybe throw it through the long stained-glass window over the couch. How long did Muriel Winter intend to keep her waiting? Didn't the woman know that she had to *work* for a living, or did her pretentious arrogance protect her from all knowledge of the real world?

Chelsea paced back and forth in front of the long table. Around her the dark oak bookshelves stretched from floor to ceiling, filled with leather-bound volumes. They looked like collectors' items and classics; she reflected sourly that they'd probably never been read. They looked supremely boring anyhow. She went over and fingered a tooled leather spine that had been stamped with gold letters. **JANE EYRE.** It was one of her favorites. She remembered reading it twice the year she was sixteen. There was something about the tenacious, patient Jane and her romance with the wealthy Mr. Rochester that had always enthralled and fascinated her.

She slid the book off the shelf and opened it. The pages were crisp with age, yet the corners had a subtly curled appearance that suggested frequent use. She flipped slowly through the book, studying the elegantly detailed illustrations. One picture in particular caught her eye: an etching of Jane in Mr. Rochester's arms. Her head was leaning on his broad chest and his face was in profile. Strands of hair hung over his forehead, and his dark eyes seemed to be regarding her with great tenderness. Chelsea felt a strange tingle in the base of her spine as she stared at the picture. Mr. Rochester bore a startling resemblance to Jeff Blaine.

She shut the book quickly and glanced at her watch. It was nearly twenty past ten. Muriel Winter had already kept her waiting for almost half an hour. It occurred to her suddenly, and with a little shock of anger, that the delay was a punishment, the calculated prelude to a scalding reprimand. Muriel had it all planned; she was going to humiliate her before she scolded her. And then she would deliberately and strategically destroy the reputation of Strawberry Lace.

I don't have to take this, she thought angrily. I was here on time. I kept the appointment. If Muriel Winter was going to insult her, she'd have to do it some other time. Chelsea straightened her shoulders, stalked to the door and yanked it open.

She gasped and stepped back into the library.

There, staring at her with a pair of narrow, ice-blue eyes, was the elegant figure of Muriel Winter. And standing right behind her, giving Chelsea the same dark-eyed smile that had first taken her breath away the day before, was Jeff Blaine.

Chapter Six

MISS ADAMS?" MURIEL EXTENDED HER hand and stepped into the library. She was just as slim and elegant as Chelsea remembered, wearing a blue sheath dress with a white jacket. Large pearl-drop earrings hung from her ears. Her dark hair was swept back gracefully from her face; her small eyes had been enlarged by makeup. Chelsea could see only a vague resemblance to Jeff, in the high forehead and full lower lip.

"Yes." Chelsea shook Muriel's hand quickly. The woman's fingers were almost icy. Not that it should be surprising. What else would she expect from someone as cold and calculating as Muriel Winter?

"You look familiar." Muriel was studying her with those small, cold eyes. "Have you done any parties for us before? I was given to understand that Strawberry Lace is a relatively new operation."

"Actually, we've been in business for three years." Chelsea was intensely aware of Jeff's gaze. He was standing quietly behind his mother, his hands loosely clasped in front of him. "Maybe you remember me from your Columbus Day cocktail party two years ago. I'm a good friend of Holly Martin."

The eyes narrowed even farther. "Holly Martin? I don't believe I recall the name."

Chelsea's back muscles tightened in anger. The woman who had ruined Holly's life didn't even remember her! She had to force herself to keep smiling. "She was engaged to your son, Brandon."

"Oh. Yes." The elegant head went up; the eyes closed very briefly; the perfect hair caught a shaft of red light from the stained-glass window. "Well, that's neither here nor there. I'm sorry to have kept you waiting." She said it without a trace of regret in her tone. It was, Chelsea realized, merely a formality, the sort of thing sophisticated people said to each other at such times. She didn't even wait for Chelsea's acknowledgment before she continued. "Certain contingencies have made it impossible for me to proceed with my initial arrangements for the Independence Day party."

Here it comes, Chelsea thought. The big brush-off. Why didn't the woman just come right out and say she was fired? Why beat around the bush with all these fancy, hundred dollar words? "Look," Chelsea said, "you don't have to spell it out. I know what's going on."

The blue eyes widened. "Excuse me?"

"I'll just leave now, so I won't waste any more of your time."

"I hardly see how that will accomplish anything." Muriel's voice was colder than ever. "And I don't possibly see how you could know the purpose of this appointment." She turned to Jeff and placed a hand on his arm. "I arrived at my decision very recently."

Chelsea noted Jeff's smile, which was laced with

mischief. Was this some trick the two of them were playing?

"Jefferson, this is Miss Adams," Muriel was saying. "You'll be working with her."

"We've already met." Jeff's grin widened.

"Working with me?" Chelsea had to tighten her jaw to keep from gaping. "But I thought you . . . I thought the party . . ."

Muriel graced her with a thin smile. "I'm turning the party supervision over to Jefferson this year. As I tried to explain, certain contingencies make it impossible for me to oversee things."

"Oh." Chelsea felt her cheeks redden. "I'm sorry. I didn't understand."

"Apparently not." Muriel gave her an indifferent stare. "Jefferson has all the information, including budget ceiling, seating arrangements, and placement of flowers. I want you to work very closely with him. I don't want any complications at this party. It must run like clockwork. Do you understand?"

"Of course. Strawberry Lace has earned its reputation, Mrs. Winter."

"I certainly hope so." Muriel nodded briefly. "I'll leave you to your deliberations, then."

As Muriel left the room, Chelsea detected a slight sway in her stride. She wondered if she'd been drinking. Was that what had delayed her this morning? A need to get enough booze into her so that she could function? She felt a shiver of disgust.

"So we meet again." Jeff was standing a few feet away, still smiling. "How are you feeling?"

"I'm fine." Chelsea faced him angrily. "Why didn't you tell me what the meeting was about? You knew all along that you were going to be in charge of this party, didn't you?"

He shoved his hands down into his pockets. "Mother mentioned something about it, yes."

"Is everything a game with you? This is the second time you've set me up!"

"I didn't set you up."

"You certainly did! Yesterday, you let me think all day long that you were the gardener. And you never even mentioned the reason for today's meeting! If I'd known you were going to be in charge, do you think I'd have spent all last night dreading this meeting, terrified that my whole business would go down the drain?"

His eyes danced. "Judging by your reaction right now, you might have been even more disturbed."

She glared, wishing she could afford to turn on her heel and walk out on the contract. If only Strawberry Lace weren't so dependent on its reputation, on the word of a few influential people. She detested the thought of working with this man.

"As far as yesterday goes," Jeff continued, "I felt complimented that you thought I was the gardener. It proves that I don't give off affluent vibrations all the time."

"And you think it's all right to just string somebody along like that, just because you feel flattered?"

His smile disappeared. "I was going to tell you, Chelsea. It's just that I enjoy remaining anonymous sometimes. It keeps people from making a lot of false assumptions about me."

"You're saying I'd have acted differently if I knew you were rich."

He smiled. "I doubt that you would have been so honest about my mother."

Her cheeks blazed.

"I didn't tell her," he said quietly. "Your opinion of her remains confidential."

It took her a minute to register his meaning. "Thanks," she mumbled. She sensed the anger draining out of her slowly and she felt a little ashamed. She'd overreacted to the situation. So Jeff Blaine had a propensity for cat and mouse games. She'd just have to stay on her toes, put the past twenty-four hours behind her and act like the professional she was. She straightened her shoulders. "Well," she said stiffly. "Perhaps we should get down to business."

"Good idea." He walked to the table and slid out a chair for her.

She sat down, took a pen and small notebook out of her purse and flipped the notebook open to the page marked *Winter*. It was already half filled with information from yesterday's tour of the estate.

Jeff sat in the chair beside her. "Where do we begin?"

"I just have a few questions."

"Ask away." He was sitting much too close to her. She could feel the warmth of his thigh under the table next to hers. His arm rested on the polished surface only millimeters from her hand.

She swallowed. "Since it's an Independence Day theme, I thought a barbecue might be appropriate. Is that agreeable?"

"Maybe you'd better spell it out."

"Well, I was thinking of a fresh clam bar, barbecued ribs, grilled chicken, lobsters, coal-roasted corn."

"Sounds good to me."

"Is it similar to what was served last year?"

"I don't see what that has to do with it."

"It's important not to repeat the theme or the menu. Strawberry Lace has a reputation for originality."

"I'm sure it does."

She sensed that he was mocking her again. "It would help if I knew what was on last year's party menu. Who catered it? What was the theme?"

He shrugged. "I have no idea. I was in Africa at the time."

"Oh." Probably he'd been on safari in Kenya. Or maybe buying diamonds in South Africa. "Well, perhaps you could get me the information."

"I'll do my best." He was smiling right at her and leaning very close. "How about dinner tonight? There's a new place on the Portland waterfront. Very classy."

She felt unexpectedly drawn to the idea and pushed it quickly away. "I'm sorry. I have a party to cater."

"Another time, then." He slid back in his chair, and Chelsea was grateful for the slight increase in distance it put between them. The scent of his cologne had left her dizzy. "So, what else do you need to know from me?"

"Nothing for the moment." She closed her notebook and stood up. "I'll be in touch."

"Good." He got to his feet and held out his hand for her to shake. She hesitated only a moment. She could hardly refrain from a handshake. This was, after all, a business arrangement.

"It's a pleasure working with you, Chelsea."

She replied without thinking, the standard response dropping out of her mouth with the promptness of habit. "The pleasure's mine."

"I'm glad to hear that." She was startled by a sudden flick of his finger across her wrist and down into her palm. Her eyes widened and she jerked her hand away quickly. When she looked up at him, his dimple had appeared and he was giving her a long, meaningful wink.

When Chelsea arrived at the Cumberland Country Club, Lori was already busy slicing cucumber rounds for the smoked trout mousse. The kitchen was large but poorly laid out, and whenever Strawberry Lace had a party at the club, they liked to do as much of the work in advance as possible. Chelsea unloaded the van, first carrying in the tins of mousse, caviar, curried chicken, and shrimp and storing them in the big stainless steel refrigerator. Then she lugged in the rest of the food and the silver serving trays that had been specially etched with the Strawberry Lace logo.

"Sorry I'm late," she said to Lori. "I'm all thumbs today for some reason. I dropped a whole box of smoked turkey just loading the van."

Lori murmured her empathy. "How did the meeting go with Mrs. Winter?"

"Oh, that." Chelsea placed a box of petits fours on the counter and stretched to ease her sore back muscles. "It seems I panicked for nothing. Apparently, Jeff didn't breathe a word to the old lady. In fact, she's put him in charge of overseeing the party."

"You're kidding! I thought Muriel Winter wouldn't let anyone touch her gala affairs."

"That's what I heard too. But it seems this time she's backing off." Chelsea opened the box and lifted out the tray of tiny sandwiches. "To tell you the truth, I think the old hag's under the influence. She could hardly walk straight this morning."

"Really?"

Chelsea nodded. "And she kept me waiting almost twenty minutes. Thankfully, though, she didn't use the drill sergeant approach I expected."

"Hmmmm." Lori started laying out the cucumber slices on a large baking sheet, ready for spreading. "I guess you must be relieved, then. Not to mention happy. Jeff seems like a real nice guy. He should be fun to work with."

"I don't know. He's got a weird sense of humor. And I think he might be the demanding type."

"Seriously? I didn't get that impression at all."

Chelsea sighed. "Frankly, I'll be relieved when the Fourth is over. I think it's going to be one big headache after another."

"You want me to be the liaison?"

"No, you don't need the aggravation. Believe me. Expose that baby to the rarefied Winter atmosphere too often and he'll be deprived of oxygen."

Lori laughed. "To tell you the truth, if I were in your shoes and still single, I'd jump at the chance to work with Jeff Blaine."

"Well, it just proves that we're nothing alike, sis. I'm not the least bit interested. Besides, I've got Stuart."

"Right. Good old Stuart."

"Which reminds me. We're going out to Eagle Island tomorrow afternoon. Do you mind making up the paté for Saturday's party on your own?"

"Not at all. Besides, I owe you one for baking the cakes last night."

"That's right. You do."

They worked feverishly through the afternoon, and by six-thirty everything was ready. The waitresses had arrived on time, four attractive college students dressed in the signature pink blouses and navy-blue skirts. The tables were set, the flower arrangements put out, and the hors d'oeuvres artistically arranged on the silver trays. It wasn't until the guests had started to arrive that Chelsea realized she'd forgotten to bring the trademark basket of strawberries.

"Oh God!" she groaned. They'd never done a party yet without their basket of strawberries. It was almost a good luck talisman. "I'd better go back for it!"

Lori shook her head. "There isn't time. Just forget it."

Chelsea sighed. "Well, let's hope the spirits don't notice." She directed the waitresses to start circulating the hors d'oeuvres trays, but the usual exhilaration she felt at the beginning of a party was gone. She only had a strong sense of dread. Something awful was going to happen. She was sure of it.

It occurred just after the petits fours had been served. Two waitresses collided with trays of red caviar, and several guests were showered with the sticky red substance. A few minutes later one of the graduates vomited into the punch bowl. Chelsea rushed to help clean up, but the damage was already done, and when the party was over, the hostess stalked into the kitchen and made her displeasure known in a shrill, penetrating voice. It was short of a stinging rebuke, but it might as well have been, as far as Chelsea was concerned. Even Lori looked stunned, which gave her normally rosy cheeks an alarming pallor. Chelsea felt sick.

"Well," Lori said, as they were loading the van, "we were bound to have a catastrophe eventually, I suppose. We're lucky to have been in business three years before our first one."

"How can you be so philosophical?" Chelsea moaned. "All that needs to happen is for word to get around that the college graduation party was a disaster and we're finished! We're looking down the wrong end of a drainpipe here."

"You're exaggerating. Besides, we'll probably be serving a whole new clientele after the Fourth of July."

"I hope you're right." Chelsea set the box of trays in the back of the van and closed the gate. "I just pray this isn't the beginning of a streak of bad luck."

"You're still drained from your big beach adventure yesterday," Lori assured her. "You'll feel better after an afternoon with Stuart."

"I hope so." Chelsea gave her sister a farewell hug and climbed into the driver's seat of the van. She had to admit, a long afternoon on the water sounded like heaven right about now.

She called Stuart as soon as she got home. When she told him what had happened at the party, he suggested she spend the whole day on *Chelsea's Choice*.

"You could come hauling with me in the morning. You haven't done that in weeks. Then we'll picnic on the island, and just play it by ear for the rest of the afternoon."

She hesitated. "I'm not sure I ought to spend the whole day."

"Come on, Chels. You know how much you love it. And how hard you've been working lately."

"Okay, but you'll have to give me a percentage of the lobster catch if you're going to put me to work."

"It's a deal."

Chelsea hung up. She smiled at the thought of spending a whole day on the water. She enjoyed hauling the big lobster traps; it was good exercise, and a break from her normal routine. The one thing she didn't like about the catering business was being trapped indoors all day.

Early the next morning, she drove out to Stuart's cedar-shingled cabin. *Chelsea's Choice* was moored in Bryant's Cove, just a few hundred yards beyond the meadow in back of his place. She could see it between the tall pines as she drove along the narrow dirt road. The water was choppy, whipped up a bit by an offshore wind, but the sky was clear and it looked like it would be a good day. She had packed a picnic lunch and brought along the mystery novel she was reading. Stuart, she knew, would be in a good mood. The price of lobster was up, and he'd had a good catch three days in a row.

She found him on the end of his sagging, wooden dock, stacking traps on his little dinghy. He was wearing faded jeans, a flannel shirt, and his beloved Red Sox baseball cap. His sun-bleached blond hair curled brightly on his neck. He looked up when he heard her footsteps on the wooden planks.

"Hey, Chels, how you doing?" He got to his feet and embraced her happily.

"Not too bad. How about helping me with the picnic things? They're in the trunk."

"Sure thing." He looped a friendly arm around her shoulder. "You look good. Not like somebody who practically drowned a couple of days ago."

"Hey, you always said I was stubborn."

He laughed and dug his fingers into her ribs, making her squeal. "You're not just stubborn, Chelsea Adams. You're downright ornery."

"And you love it. Isn't that why we have such a good, no-pressure relationship?"

His expression sobered. "Yeah, well, that's something we need to talk about. No pressure's one thing. No commitment's another."

She shaded her eyes against the glint of sunlight off the water so she could read his expression. "You sound like you've been talking to Lori. What exactly are you saying?"

"Don't get excited. It's just some stuff I've been thinking about. We can talk later."

They carried the picnic things down to the dinghy and rowed out to *Chelsea's Choice* without speaking. Chelsea was so used to doing her own chores aboard the boat that she didn't have to ask Stuart what he wanted done. She just went straight to work, stowing the food in the little cabin, pulling on the pair of waterproof overalls Stuart kept on board for her use, helping him stack his wire traps in the *Chelsea*'s spacious stern. It was almost like dancing, moving this way to the rhythm of the tide.

Stuart ducked into the cockpit to start the engine, and its thunderous roar drowned out any hope of conversation. Chelsea settled down with her novel on a box pushed up against the washboards.

Stuart turned the boat and headed out, running fast through the cove's deep central channel. The wind whipped Chelsea's hair around her face, so that she had to keep pushing it out of her eyes. Stuart was heading out to his favorite fishing spot; it was off one of the little islands that dotted Casco Bay like green jewels this time of year. It would take a while to get there.

She was thoroughly absorbed in her book when Stuart cut the engine and started baiting traps. She helped him fasten the fat, foul-smelling bait bags inside and then stood watching as he slid the weighted traps overboard one by one. The warp line ran out fast as the traps dropped into the water. He handed her the brightly painted purple and white buoy, and she tossed it into the water. Then he turned the boat and went after an identical buoy bobbing on the choppy water a few hundred yards away. Reaching it, he cut the engine, hooked the buoy aboard with a long metal gaff pole, tugged the line into the hydraulic winch, and started it up. The line of traps rose slowly, dripping seaweed and water in the bright sun. Chelsea always felt a little thrill at the sight of a new trap coming aboard. It was like being a child again, presented with a birthday present; you never knew what it might contain. She helped Stuart slide the traps onto the washboard and unfasten the little wire doors. Three of the traps held good-sized lobsters, which Stuart dropped into the tub of seawater at his feet. He was grinning as they rebaited the traps and slid them away.

"Looks like another good day," he told her as he started the engine again. "My lucky streak seems to be holding."

When they finished hauling, Stuart headed *Chelsea's Choice* out to Eagle Island. It was a spot that Chelsea had always loved, and she was a little sad that tourists had discovered it recently. The large summer home of the Arctic explorer Robert Peary rode the northern tip of the little island like the prow of a great ship. They moored off the small beach, stowed the picnic things aboard the skiff, and rowed in.

Gulls wheeled overhead in the bright blue sky. Chelsea was relieved to note that there were only two other boats riding the swells. It meant they had the island pretty much to themselves.

They ate on a sun-warmed boulder overlooking the beach. Chelsea had the strange feeling that Stuart was watching her closely throughout the meal, but every time she glanced at him, he was surveying the water. It wasn't until they were finished and Chelsea was stretching out to soak up the delicious warmth of the sun that he stunned her with his declaration.

"Chelsea," he said in a tone so ardent that she almost didn't recognize it as his, "I think it's time we got married."

Chapter Seven

CHELSEA SAT UP ABRUPTLY. "WHAT DID you say?"

"I said, I think it's time we got married." Stuart took her hand, very tenderly, in his. "We've known each other for almost ten years now, Chels. We have a great relationship. Neither of us is interested in seeing anyone else. We belong together."

She blinked at him. The pressure of his fingers on her skin moved her. He leaned closer, his blue eyes bright with ardor, and she realized, suddenly, that he was going to kiss her.

"Stuart—wait a minute. I thought we both agreed—"

He cut her off. "I want a family. A wife and kids to come home to. I'm going to be thirty next year. I'm tired of bachelor life." He reached for her again, pulled her into his arms. "Come on, Chels, you know we're perfect together. It's not as if we've never talked about this."

"But I didn't think we were ever that serious. I mean, our relationship isn't exactly passionate or anything."

His blue eyes darkened. "That can change," he said softly. He cupped her cheek gently, let his fingers slide down the length of her neck to the soft indendation above the collarbone. "Chels, I love you. I want to marry you. You know we're meant for each other."

He kissed her, his lips molding hers tenderly. She felt a peaceful warmth flow through her as she closed her eyes and kissed him back. When he finally released her, all she could do was gape at him in surprise.

"How long have you been feeling this way?" she asked. "When did things change?"

He smiled. "I'm not sure anything's changed. I've always known there was something very special between us. My feelings for you run very deep. In the past few weeks I've just realized that it's more than a friendship. Much more. I can't imagine life without you."

"But why should you have to?"

"Because, Chels, if you don't marry me, some tall handsome prince is going to ride into Maynard Landing one day and carry you off. And I don't want that to happen. Ever."

Chelsea tried to absorb the import of what had just happened. For years she had regarded Stuart with admiration, warmth, and a unique fondness. Now, within a few seconds, all that had changed.

"I don't know what to say," she murmured.

"How about yes?"

She blew out a long breath and stared down at her hands. They looked long and pale against the dark blue denim of her jeans. "I'm just so stunned. I thought everything was fine between us."

He chuckled. "It is, Chels. It's perfect. That's why I'm asking you."

"You're really serious about this, aren't you?"

He nodded solemnly.

"Well." She gave him a quick smile and got to her feet, brushing her hands on the back of her jeans. "You're going to have to give me a few minutes to let it sink in. Let's take a walk around the island, okay?"

"Sure." He got up and carried the picnic things back to the dinghy. She watched his muscular stride up the beach toward her, his blond hair tossing in the wind, his confident smile as he gazed at her. He'd do anything for her, she knew. He was devoted to her, had been from the minute they'd first met. He'd been a high school senior then and she an insecure, morose sophomore, still trying to make sense of her father's death. Stuart had been the answer to all her prayers. She'd never looked at any other boys, never even *wanted* to, except for that brief period in college. She loved him the way she would have loved a brother, if she'd had one. She couldn't imagine *not* loving him.

She slid off the rock and together they started along the narrow path that circled the island. The foliage was a profusion of green. Tiny wildflowers lined the edges of the wooded trail. Chelsea spotted several patches of still-green wild strawberries hidden in the underbrush. They stopped to sit on a granite outcropping and gaze out to sea. She wasn't surprised that Stuart didn't press her on the issue of marriage; it wasn't his style. His composure gave her time to seriously consider his proposal. The thought of being Stuart's wife, of living with him for the rest of her life, was appealing. There was no one in the world she liked better. The more she thought about it, the more she realized that marrying Stuart had been her destiny from the beginning.

So it was with a sense of inevitability and a great tenderness that she turned to him as they came out of the woods behind the house.

"Of course I'll marry you, Stuart," she said, putting her arms around him and kissing him happily. "How could I say no to the most wonderful man on earth?"

There was a call waiting on her answering machine when Chelsea got back to her apartment. She assumed it was Lori, letting her know that the paté had come out perfectly, so she was startled to hear the sound of Jeff Blaine's voice resonating through her living room.

"Chelsea, this is Jeff. We've run into some problems on the party. I need to see you ASAP." There was a little click as he hung up.

She ran the message again, wondering what problem could be so urgent that it demanded an unscheduled meeting. She hadn't even thought about the Independence Day party today, nor would she be likely to put much thought into it for the next week or so; it was over a month away, and she had half a dozen affairs to cater first.

In any case, she had to think about her wedding. Stuart was already pressing her to set a date. He wanted her to rent out her apartment and move into his cabin before fall. He'd told her so as he was rowing into shore from the *Chelsea*'s mooring in Bryant's Cove.

"I'm still getting used to the idea of being engaged," she'd said, laughing. But he wasn't about to be distracted.

"Mid-July at the absolute latest," he said. "I'll get you an engagement ring tomorrow. It won't be anything fancy, but it won't be so tiny it'll embarrass you." He was backing with his oars, slowing the dinghy so it would bump gently against the dock.

"There's no need to get a ring. We both know we're engaged. That's all that's important, isn't it?" She'd leaned her head against his muscular forearm. "Besides, you need to save your money for a new engine. *Chelsea's Choice* isn't going to hold out much longer."

He jumped lightly onto the dock, pulled hard on the line so that the skiff swung sideways, and tied it to the ring, then gave Chelsea a hand up. "That's true." He put his arms around her. "Are you sure? I want to do right by you, Chels. I don't want you to feel cheated."

"How could I feel cheated? I'm the luckiest woman in the world!" She'd kissed him and started up the path to the cabin. "Come on, let's go get a cup of hot coffee. I'm chilled right through to the bone."

They'd embraced in his immaculate little kitchen, his hands wandering sensuously over her body. She'd expected the shiver of arousal that was supposed to come with such intimacies, and had been surprised when she'd felt nothing but a familiar fondness. The problem, she realized, as she headed back to her apartment, was that she was too used to thinking of Stuart as a friend. It would take her a little while to see him as a lover.

She carried the remains of the picnic lunch into the kitchen and rinsed off the plastic dishes and silverware. She wondered if Jeff wanted her to call him right away. ASAP could mean anything from immediately to a couple of days. Her curiosity grew as she wiped down the counters and fixed the coffee machine for her morning wake-up cup. It was only nine o'clock; not too late to call. She flicked off the light in the kitchen, went into the living room and turned on the TV.

She flipped through the channels, but nothing interested her. For some odd reason, all she could think about was Jeff's phone call.

She forced her mind back to the events of the day. What she should do was call Lori and her mother and tell them she was engaged. Her mother would be delighted and eager to hear all the details. Lori was another matter; her first reaction would probably be to laugh. She'd been convinced for years that Stuart wasn't right for her, that her relationship with him was holding her back from meeting other men. They'd had long arguments about it, but no amount of certainty on Chelsea's part could change Lori's mind.

Chelsea remembered the most recent discussion on the subject, which had taken place just last Saturday, while they were making Salade Nicoise for a twenty-fifth anniversary luncheon. Lori had insisted that she should stop seeing Stuart. "You need somebody who can't be pushed around, Chels. Stuart's too good-natured for you."

"Oh, thanks a lot," Chelsea had snapped. "I suppose you want me to find some hairy macho type who rules his woman with an iron hand."

"No, but I do think you need to find someone who's at least as bullheaded as you are."

"Stuart has a mind of his own."

Lori had given her a sad smile. "Not where you're

concerned, Chels. He's been wrapped around your little finger since the day you first met him."

The phone rang, startling Chelsea out of her recollection. She flicked off the TV, stretched the length of the couch to grab the receiver out of its cradle.

"Strawberry Lace."

"Chelsea?" It was Jeff. "I'm glad I caught you. Did you get my message?"

"Yes, I did. I was going to call in the morning."

"It can't wait. I need to see you tonight."

"Tonight?"

"Yes. Do you mind if I come by?"

She hesitated.

"It's very important."

"Okay. I guess it would be all right." She wondered why she felt that funny little stomach flutter every time she heard his voice. "Can you tell me what this is about?"

"I'm on my way," was all he said. And then the line clicked and went dead.

"Damn!" She jammed the receiver back into its cradle and rubbed her forehead with her fingers. Why had she given in so easily? After a whole day on the water, she was tired; she needed sleep. Or at least a relaxing evening alone. She certainly didn't need a mysterious meeting with a wealthy, egotistical playboy.

Well, there wasn't anything she could do about it now. Jeff was already on his way. If she hurried, she had just enough time for a quick shower to wash the salt out of her hair.

She was toweling off in the bathroom when she heard the doorbell. Damn, she thought. How could he have come all the way from the Winter estate in such a short time? He must have driven like a pilot from Hell.

"Just a minute," she called. She hung the towel, slipped into her bathrobe, and went to answer the door.

Jeff was wearing khaki slacks and a teal-blue sweatshirt. His expression was solemn as he stepped into the room.

"I'm afraid you caught me in the shower," she said. "If you'll give me a minute, I'll be right with you. Just make yourself at home." She started toward the bedroom.

"No, don't bother." He caught her arm and pulled her around to face him. "You look fine. Anyway, this won't take long. But it's very important."

She felt distinctly uneasy, standing there wearing only her bathrobe. But Jeff's face seemed so full of raw urgency that she relented. "What is it?" She sat down gingerly in the easy chair, tucking the front of her robe tightly around her legs.

He sat opposite her on the couch, a portrait of tension, his back inclined forward, his hands massaging each other between his knees. His dark eyes were shadowed. "My mother's changed her mind about the party. She wants to call it off."

Her stomach clenched. "Because of me?"

"No. Personal reasons. She doesn't think she can handle it."

"Oh. I'm sorry. I was looking forward to catering it."

"The thing is, I want her to go ahead with it. I think it's important for her morale. She's"—he hesitated, spread his hands,—"she's going through a difficult time right now. But I believe she needs to keep up her social contacts. And her Independence Day party is the event of the season."

Chelsea nodded slowly. "So what are you suggesting?"

"I'm not exactly sure. I was hoping you might have some ideas. Have you ever dealt with a similar problem?"

She shook her head. "Have you talked to her about it? Told her your feelings?"

"Yes. She claims her mind is made up." He gave her a slight smile. "I should warn you, she's somewhat inflexible at times."

That was putting it mildly. From everything she'd heard, Muriel Winter was as unyielding as a brick wall. Chelsea shrugged. "Well, maybe you could throw a little surprise party for her—just a small cocktail party or something—then she'd realize she could handle the bigger affair on the Fourth."

His face brightened. "What a great idea! Why didn't I think of that?" He jumped up, and before she could stop him, he'd reached down and plucked her hands off her knee, where they'd been keeping her bathrobe closed. As he squeezed them warmly between his, the lower flap of her bathrobe slid open, revealing the entire length of her legs. She yanked her hands out of his and quickly covered herself. But she was certain, from the glint in his dark eyes, that he'd caught a glimpse of her inner thigh.

She was blushing furiously as she fought to regain her composure. "Then I take it you'd like Strawberry Lace to arrange a small party," she said in a choked voice.

"Yes. Definitely." He took a step backward and swept a lock of hair off his forehead. "I apologize for . . ." She saw that his own face had reddened slightly. ". . . for disturbing you," he finished. "But I appreciate your help. Really."

"That's okay." His embarrassment was touching; it exposed a vulnerable side of him she hadn't seen, one she hadn't even imagined. "I'll draw up some plans and get back to you." She stood and crossed to her desk, where she opened her appointment book. "I have a couple of free dates in the middle of June. Would the fourteenth be all right?"

"Sounds good to me."

"You'll need to get me a guest list as soon as possible. About fifteen or twenty people."

"No problem. I'll have it in your hands tomorrow morning."

"Great." She closed the book and turned to face him. He was gazing at her with a strange expression. "Is something wrong?"

"No." He shook his head as if to clear it. "No, not at all. Everything's fine now."

She called Lori as soon as he left.

"But the fourteenth is less than a month away!" Lori wailed. "And we don't even have a menu planned yet!"

"We've done it before, in less time," Chelsea reminded her.

"Not for Muriel Winter!"

"It was either that or the whole deal is off. I figured it was worth a shot."

Lori sighed. "I guess you're right. But you know how those little cocktail parties are. Everyone's got their eye on everybody else. Including *us.*"

"I'll remember the strawberries this time, don't worry. I've learned my lesson."

She was relieved to hear Lori laugh. "So when do we start planning?"

"Tomorrow, I guess. Right after the Tegram's graduation party."

The conversation shifted to the details of the next day's affair, and it wasn't until long after Chelsea had hung up that she realized she hadn't even mentioned her engagement.

Chelsea was in the shop early the next morning, assembling the three-tiered graduation cake for the Tegram's party, when she heard the shop door chime open. She wiped her hands on her apron and went out to the office, where she found Jeff Blaine leaning across the display counter, waving a long white envelope.

"The guest list," he announced, handing it to her. "I really appreciate your taking this on with so little notice."

"It's no problem." She took the envelope, opened it and glanced at the list of names. "Would you like to choose the invitations while you're here?"

He shrugged. "I'll leave them to your judgment. I would like to check over the menu, though, when you have it ready."

"Of course."

"Price is no object."

She nodded. That went without saying, considering where the party was being held.

"And I don't want you to hesitate to call if you need anything." He leaned farther over the counter, bringing his face close to hers. "Anything at all."

"I'll do that." She could smell his cologne. A spicy musk, very seductive.

He straightened, splayed his hands on the

counter. "Have you had any aftereffects from your little adventure at the beach?"

"No, I've been fine."

"Good. You're lucky. I still think I should have taken you to a hospital."

"I've been around the water all my life. A few minutes in the ocean wasn't going to hurt me."

His expression turned serious. "You hit your head. And it was more than a few minutes. You were in serious danger."

"I realize that," she said stiffly. She hated being lectured. Especially by someone who had spent his whole life wrapped in the cocoon of wealth and privilege. "And I appreciate your help."

"I'm not asking for gratitude. I just want to be sure you didn't suffer any head trauma."

"I told you, I'm fine." She snapped the envelope down into the pocket of her apron. "You'll have to excuse me. I have work to do."

He nodded. " 'Work brings its own relief.' "

"What's that supposed to mean?"

He grinned. "It's a quote. Eugene Fitch Ware. It just popped into my head for some reason." He tapped the top of the counter lightly. "Look, I'll get out of here. Let me know when you have the menu ready for the surprise party."

"I will. I should have that finished by Monday at the latest."

"Good." He smiled, a full, open smile that showed his dimple. Her response took her by surprise: an immediate, acute throb of desire, crashing like a storm wave against the ridges of her spine.

Chapter Eight

THE TEGRAM'S GRADUATION PARTY WENT like clockwork. The guests raved about the lavish flower arrangements, the graduation cake, and the colorful array of finger foods.

"We're back in business," Lori sang, peering through a window as the last of the guests left the stately Tegram home. It was after midnight, and the cloud cover was so thick there were no visible stars. The weatherman had predicted that the rain would hold off for another twenty-four hours, but Chelsea doubted it.

"I hope so." Chelsea took a disheartened look around the cluttered kitchen. They still had clean-up to do before leaving, which meant she wouldn't be home before two. "Let's get going, Lori. I don't want to be up all night. I have to take Mom to Sunday dinner tomorrow." She sighed and started stacking baking sheets and plates.

"You want me to do it? Paul and I wouldn't mind having her come to our place again." Lori seemed surprisingly energetic, considering her pregnancy and the late hour.

"No, it's my turn. Besides, I've got some news she'll want to hear."

"You mean the Winter party?" Lori turned from the sink, where she was rinsing plates for the dishwasher. "I already told her, Chels. I'm sorry if I stole your thunder."

"No, this is something else." She carried the stack of trays to the counter beside the sink. "Stuart and I are getting married."

"You're kidding."

"No, we just decided yesterday."

Lori let the dish she was holding clatter into the sink. "You're making a huge mistake."

"I *knew* you'd say that!" Chelsea opened the dishwasher, grabbed a handful of silverware from the counter and shoved it into its basket.

"Well, good grief, Chels, what am I supposed to say? You know how I feel. There's no spark between you; you've told me that yourself. Just a whole lot of convenience."

"There's a lot more than convenience between Stuart and me! Anyway, convenience isn't a crime!"

"No, but it's not a good basis for marriage."

"Just because you've been married for three years doesn't make you an expert on the subject. Your marriage to Paul hasn't exactly been problem-free."

"That's true, but at least we're in love with each other. That's helped us over more than a few bad spots."

"Who says I'm not in love with Stuart?"

"You did, Chels. A long time ago. And I haven't seen any evidence to contradict it."

"Then you haven't been paying attention. Feelings can change, you know." Chelsea measured soap into the dishwasher and closed the heavy metal door.

"Besides, you're not the only woman in the world who wants to have children, sis. Stuart's a wonderful guy, and he wants to marry me. It's not as if there's a line waiting at my door. There aren't too many eligible bachelors out there."

"Maybe *you're* the one who's not paying attention," Lori said softly.

"What's that supposed to mean?"

"I saw the way Jeff Blaine looked at you the other day. And he's about as eligible as they come."

"Jeff Blaine? You must be kidding! I wouldn't go *near* a son of Muriel Winter's after what happened to Holly!"

"Jeff isn't Brandon."

"He's still Muriel Winter's son."

Lori sighed. "Okay, bury your head in the sand if you want to. Go ahead and marry Stuart. I just think you're making a mistake."

"You've made that very clear."

They finished the clean-up in rapid silence, driven by their tension. It was a cleansing process, one they had resorted to often over the years after their sisterly spats. Chelsea felt her anger leak away gradually, and by the time the van was loaded, it was gone.

A few raindrops spattered the windshield as she pulled into Lori's driveway. Chelsea gave her sister a warm good-bye hug and waited until Lori was safely inside before leaving. The unwelcome drizzle irritated her. It was likely to develop into a downpour, and she hated driving in the rain. Especially this late at night. Lori's house was almost half an hour from the shop. She always worried that the van would break down and leave her stranded, miles from home.

She decided to take a shortcut. It was a route she'd

driven a few times in daylight, but the inky nighttime blackness transformed the narrow, tree-lined road into a winding, black tunnel. She drove carefully, alert for the deer and raccoons that might be venturing across the road. The windshield wipers slid back and forth in a constant, drowsy rhythm. Fatigue drifted through her in waves; her eyelids grew heavy. She fought to stay awake, but the rain-blurred glow of headlights under the trees was trance-inducing. She slapped her face with her hand a couple of times, to force herself back to vigilance.

It wasn't until she recognized the same dilapidated barn looming up on her right, which she'd passed only a short time before, that she realized she was lost. She scolded herself for not paying attention and tried to get her bearings. The landmarks she could make out in the darkness looked familiar, but she didn't know if that was because she'd just passed them or because she was on the right road. She kept going, fully awake now, berating herself for her stupidity. Even so, she didn't see the deer until it was almost too late.

He leaped out of the woods on her right, just a few hundred feet in front of the van. Instead of continuing across the road, he turned his magnificent antlered head toward her headlights and froze.

She stamped on the brakes and swerved hard to the left. The resulting screech seemed to release the buck from his spell, and he darted away into the trees. But it was too late for Chelsea. The van skidded, swayed, and plunged into the deep ditch on the far side of the road. It tilted far to the right and for one horrifying moment seemed about to roll over. Then it rocked back and settled into the ditch, its engine still grinding loudly, as if to protest its misfortune.

She turned off the ignition and sat for a moment in darkness, listening to the rain beat on the metal roof, waiting for her heart to stop slamming against her ribs. It had been a narrow escape. She was lucky the van wasn't totaled, lucky to be alive.

She climbed out and tried to assess the damage by the light of the headlights. Rain poured down, drenching her hair and clothes, saturating her pink blouse so that it stuck to her skin. From what she could see, the van appeared intact. But it was definitely stuck. The sides of the ditch were steep and stubbled with rocks and brambles. She'd have to have the van towed out.

She glanced at her watch. One forty-five. She hadn't passed a house in some time, it was pouring rain, and there didn't seem to be any traffic at all on the road. Her best bet was probably to sleep in the van and walk out in the morning. It might be miles before she came to a dwelling, but at least she'd be able to see where she was heading. And if there was morning traffic on the road, which seemed likely, she could hail someone for help.

She was opening the van door to climb back inside when she heard the sound of an engine in the distance. Her heart gave a little leap of hope. She scrambled up the slippery ditch to the roadside, straining her ears to listen. It was definitely a car, and it seemed to be headed her way. After a few minutes she could even see the ripple of headlights through the trees.

Finally, the car rounded the curve at the top of the hill. Chelsea shouted and jumped into the road, waving her arms. She was instantly blinded by the headlights. Just like the buck, she thought, and made herself step back onto the shoulder. The car slowed and pulled to a stop a few feet away.

It was only then, squinting and shading her eyes to peer through the driving rain, that it occurred to her what a hazardous position she was in. She sent up a small prayer that the driver was a sane, nonviolent person, not some psychotic killer on the loose. She braced herself, ready to sprint down the slope and lock herself into the van at the first hint of danger.

The car door opened and a man emerged. She couldn't make out his features because of the rain and the glaring headlights, but his height and the broad slant of his shoulders were vaguely familiar.

"Is that you, Chelsea?"

"Jeff!" She felt her knees wobble as she let the air go out of her in a long breath. "Thank God you came by!" She started toward him and then stopped as the passenger door opened and Beth Harmon got out.

"Are you okay?" Beth called.

Chelsea nodded dumbly as she watched Jeff and Beth come toward her. As they stepped in front of the car, her glance went quickly to Beth's black low-cut dress, then flicked to Jeff's immaculately tailored suit.

"Are you okay?" Beth repeated.

"My . . . my van's down there," she finally managed to gasp. She motioned toward the ditch. "I tried to avoid a deer and went over."

Jeff was already scrambling down the ditch slope before she could warn him about the brambles. Beth put a hand on her arm. "Come on and get in the car before you get pneumonia."

Chelsea shook her head numbly, strangely unable

to move. Then Jeff was beside her, pushing something into her hands, which she recognized dully as her purse. "Looks like you're going to have to leave the van here for the night." He rubbed his hands to brush them clean. "I turned off your lights and locked it up for you. I'll give you a ride to your place."

"Thanks, but I don't want to inconvenience you."

"Don't be silly," Beth said. "It's pouring. We're not going to leave you stranded here. Come on, get in the car."

Chelsea climbed reluctantly into the backseat. Beth handed her a black crocheted shawl. "It's not much, but it's better than nothing. Wrap it around you until we get to your place." Chelsea obeyed, clumsily pulling the shawl around her shoulders. Jeff flicked on the inside lights and turned in the driver's seat to study Chelsea.

"You sure you're not hurt?"

"I'm fine."

"No hospital, right?" He grinned.

She nodded.

He pulled the car back onto the road, did a three-point turn, and headed back the way he'd come. Chelsea sat hunched in a corner of the seat, tasting her humiliation as a bitter coating on the back of her tongue. She was soaking the backseat of Jeff's car. Her legs and arms were scratched with brambles; all her makeup had washed off. She knew she looked terrible, especially compared to the beautifully dressed Beth.

They had only traveled a few miles before they reached a familiar Mobil station on an otherwise deserted corner. Jeff turned right, and within minutes he was pulling up in front of Strawberry Lace.

"Thanks a million," Chelsea said. "I'm sorry to put you to so much trouble." She scrambled out of the car and ran for the stairway door.

She was startled to find Jeff right behind her as she hurried up the stairs. He didn't say anything, but when she unlocked the door, he reached past her to push it open and flick on the overhead light.

"I really don't need an escort," she said. "But thanks." She was too tired and too shaken to be able to construct a fancy speech of appreciation.

He grinned. "Seems like you're a regular damsel in distress, Chelsea Adams."

"If you're implying I'm the helpless type—"

"Not at all. But maybe just a wee bit accident prone."

Her cheeks flared. "I had no idea you'd be coming along that particular road at two in the morning . . ." She saw his dimple appear, and felt a responsive flutter. It dawned on her that she was just making his case for him. "I'm glad you did, though," she admitted.

He squeezed her shoulder lightly. "Get some sleep."

And then he was gone, jogging down the stairs and swinging through the door at the bottom. Going back to Beth, Chelsea thought with a little throb of jealousy, then caught herself.

She didn't care who Jeff Blaine spent his time with. Her only involvement with him was a business relationship.

She went into the apartment and locked the door behind her. Moments later she was tucked down under the covers of her bed, sleeping the sweet, oblivious sleep of exhaustion.

* * *

Chelsea slept until ten Sunday morning, and when she woke, it took her a few minutes to remember the events of the night before. The memory of Jeff Blaine smiling at her was the strongest impression that remained; everything else seemed dark and nightmarish. She called the towing service before she showered, and by the time she'd finished her morning coffee, the van was back in her driveway and the bill paid.

She took the Toyota up I-95 to Yarmouth. She usually looked forward to the bimonthly Sunday luncheons with her mother, but today the prospect of explaining her engagement, as well as last night's accident, seemed like an ordeal. Her mother would ask a million questions, especially when it came to marriage. Her mother liked Stuart, but found him dull. Not that her mother's choice in men had been a wonderful model. She was a born romantic. After Chelsea's father died, she'd fallen for a handsome real estate broker from Portland and married him following a whirlwind courtship, only to discover, fifteen months later, that he had another wife in New Hampshire. She'd been only temporarily devastated, immediately falling in love again and marrying a man who was a dedicated gambler. He drained her entire savings account in two years. After her second divorce, Chelsea had questioned her about the wisdom of remarriage, and her mother had admitted that it probably wasn't a great idea.

"Three strikes and you're out," she'd said morosely, and then brightened to tell Chelsea about a new man she'd met at the senior center. "He's so exciting! It was love at first sight! Would you believe he's been to the Australian outback?"

Chelsea had shaken her head inwardly, and given

up the fight. Her mother had to live her own life. Her mother would never understand her relationship with Stuart. Probably because she'd never had such a good, solid relationship with a man.

Her mother was weeding the tiny flower garden in front of her duplex when Chelsea pulled up. She was dressed in baggy slacks and a sweatshirt, with a pink bandanna wrapped around her short white hair.

"I thought we were going out to eat!" Chelsea complained. "Did you forget this is my Sunday?"

Her mother turned a luminous smile on her. "Yes, dear, I know. But I'm *so* tired of eating restaurant food. Bill's taken me dining and dancing every night this week. Do you mind if we just stay here?"

So they ate crabmeat sandwiches in her mother's tiny kitchen while Chelsea related the details of Stuart's proposal. She was relieved that her mother didn't seem as curious as she'd expected. All she really wanted to talk about was her own budding romance with the guy who'd been to Australia.

Chelsea listened as patiently as she could until her mother suggested, with a twinkle in her blue eyes, that she and Chelsea might want to consider a double ceremony.

"You mean Bill's proposed to you already?"

"Not yet. But he's going to. What do you think—should we tie the knot together?"

Chelsea wiped her mouth again with the crumpled paper napkin. "I think I'd like my own wedding, Mom."

"I understand perfectly, dear. How are things going with the business?"

"Pretty good, actually. We're doing the Fourth of July for Muriel Winter."

"Muriel *Winter!* How wonderful!" Her mother lowered her voice confidentially, as if they were in a restaurant and might be overheard by other people. "Do you think you could arrange an invitation for Bill and me?"

"You know I can't do that kind of thing."

"I was just asking. I hear the Winter estate is really spectacular. Maybe I could help in the kitchen that night, just to get a peek."

"Absolutely not!"

"Well, it doesn't hurt to ask. Have you met Muriel yet?"

"Once. Actually, her son's supervising all the party arrangements."

"Brandon's back from England?"

"Not Brandon. She has another son by her first marriage. His name's Jeff Blaine."

"I'd heard she was married before, but I didn't think there were any children. She was pretty young when her first husband died."

"Well, I don't know the details, except that he's her son and he's the person I'm working with."

Her mother's eyes sparkled. "What does he look like? Is he handsome?"

"I suppose so, in a fashion-magazine kind of way. He's tall, has dark hair and brown eyes." She was startled by the odd little ripple of excitement in her chest as she mentally pictured Jeff. She shrugged it quickly away.

"What does he do? For work, I mean?"

"I don't expect he does anything except travel around the world. He said something about being in Africa last year."

"How exciting! Wouldn't you just love to see Africa?"

"Not particularly. I like it here. Anyway, you know

I have a job that I adore. And which is more important to me than all the money and leisure time in the world."

"Don't get huffy. I was just thinking how nice—"

"I know what you were thinking, Mom. And I'm perfectly happy with my life. Just the way it is. Fiancé and all."

"If you say so, Chelsea." She stood and picked up her plate. "What shall we do this afternoon? How about a walk down by the marina?"

"Sounds good to me." Chelsea carried her own plate to the sink. The entire length of her spine felt tight, as if the disks had locked together like cold, metal couplings.

They spent the afternoon watching sailboats ply the water of the Royal River. The sails caught the sunlight like triangles crayoned by a child in radiant colors. Chelsea wondered what it would be like to have enough money to own a sailboat. There was something magical about seeing the bright sails under the high blue sky.

She walked her mother back to her house and gave her a warm good-bye hug before she left. She felt relaxed and refreshed. The walk and the fresh salt air had done her good. As she headed south again on the interstate, she found herself singing along with the radio. But all the way home, for some strange reason, her mind kept pulling up images of Jeff Blaine. He was smiling down at her, his dark eyes sparkling and his long dimple showing. And she was smiling back.

Chapter Nine

CHELSEA WOKE TO THE INSISTENT RING of the telephone. Startled, she rolled over and snatched the receiver out of its cradle on her bedside table. The clock read seven-thirty. Who on earth was calling this early in the morning?

"Hello? Strawberry Lace."

"Chelsea? Hope I didn't wake you." The instant she heard Jeff's voice, she remembered her promise. She'd assured him she'd come up with a menu for the surprise party, but she hadn't done a thing, hadn't even *thought* about it all weekend.

"No," she said quickly. "I'm awake. What can I do for you?"

"I need to change the date of the surprise party. Move it up to June seventh. Can you do that?"

She almost gasped. "The seventh? That's less than two weeks away!"

"I know. But my mother's going to Boston on the tenth. And I'd really like to have the party before she leaves."

She hesitated. "I'm just not sure—"

"I'll help. You can even put me to work in the

kitchen, if you like." His tone lowered, became strangely intimate. "Please. I wouldn't ask if it weren't important."

Chelsea's stomach fluttered. "Okay, I'll try."

"Good. Would it help if I came down and approved the menu right now?"

"No . . . I . . ." She swallowed. "To tell you the truth, I haven't figured it out yet."

"No problem. I have some ideas. We can make plans this morning."

"I'm not sure—"

"Over breakfast at the Seacroft Inn. My treat."

"The Seacroft Inn!"

"Yes. They serve a great breakfast buffet there. Have you ever sampled their currant scones?"

"No, but I've heard about them." The Seacroft was one of the most exclusive restaurants on the coast of Maine. It was actually a resort, with private dining rooms and intimate lounges, even a library. She'd never gone there, had only caught glimpses of the stately stone mansion set on wide, rolling lawns overlooking the ocean. But she'd always dreamed of dining at the Seacroft. Just once before she died, she promised herself, she'd sit by one of those tall, leaded glass windows, with the candlelight glowing on her hair, and gaze out to sea.

"You'll love them, I promise."

"I appreciate your offer." She tried to sound calm and professional but her heart was pounding much too hard and her chest felt constricted. "But I usually do the planning with my sister, and she doesn't work mornings."

"That's all right. I'm sure, between the two of us, we can come up with something interesting."

"Jeff, I—"

"You want to go. I can hear it in your voice."

"What I want and what's good for Strawberry Lace are two separate things."

"I'll pick you up in twenty minutes." He hung up before she could get in another word.

Chelsea sat for a moment, staring at the receiver in her hand. She felt a little dizzy. She'd never met anyone quite so self-confident and assertive. Except for Muriel Winter. Jeff certainly came by his forcefulness honestly. She wondered if dealing with the very rich was always like this. Did you always feel like nothing more than a cog in a wheel, manipulated for the other person's convenience? Wasn't that how people became wealthy in the first place? By using other people? Well, she'd have to put up with it for the sake of the business. But that didn't mean she had to like it.

Chelsea showered and dressed quickly in a simple black dress. She clipped a string of false pearls around her neck and draped her lime-green cardigan over her shoulders. After sliding into a pair of black heels, she piled her hair into a loose knot on the top of her head and secured it with combs. She checked herself in the mirror at least a dozen times, wondering if she looked elegant enough for the Seacroft, finally resigning herself to the fact that she probably didn't and never would, given her present budget. The sound of Jeff's car pulling up to the curb in front of the apartment made her scurry to locate her menu planning books and hurry down the stairs so he wouldn't have to climb them.

She burst through the door onto the sidewalk and was surprised to find him wearing comfortable slacks and a casual knit shirt. She realized with a little start of horror that she was overdressed.

"Should I change?" she asked faintly.

His eyes roved quickly over her body and came back to her face. "Absolutely not. You look terrific." He opened the passenger door for her.

She climbed in, clutching the notebooks against her breasts, and it was only when he was beside her and snapping his seat belt around him that she remembered hers. In the process of putting it on, Chelsea released the notebooks and they fell to the floor. As she leaned forward to retrieve them, he reached for them as well, and her hand inadvertently brushed his. She felt an electric tingle travel up her arm to her shoulder.

When she looked up, he was smiling at her, his dark eyes shining with an expression that told her he knew exactly what she was feeling. That he was feeling the same thing.

The Seacroft was even more elegant than she'd imagined. Subdued blue and rose Oriental carpets covered the floors; the walls were paneled in richly carved oak; tapestries hung from the vaulted ceilings. As they entered the foyer, it was all Chelsea could do not to stop and gape up at the ornate chandeliers.

There were only three other diners in the breakfast room: an elderly couple sitting next to the massive marble fireplace, and a middle-aged woman immersed in the *New York Times*. A waiter, immaculately attired in a white dress shirt and black slacks, escorted Chelsea and Jeff to a small table near a bay window overlooking the ocean. Chelsea tried to slide her notebooks inconspicuously under her chair, but the waiter picked them up and offered to set them aside for her.

"I don't know—" She hesitated and glanced at Jeff.

"Take them, by all means," Jeff said to the waiter. "We'll let you know when we need them."

The waiter nodded and disappeared.

"Why did you do that?" She felt as if her voice were strangely muffled in the huge room. Maybe it was just the intimidating surroundings.

"He'll bring them to us any time we want them," Jeff said quietly. He picked up his plate. "Shall we eat?"

They headed for the far end of the room, where a buffet table was laid out in front of tall, leaded windows. The array of food was staggering. The table was covered with baskets of croissants, muffins, and biscuits; trays of baked ham slices and tiny sausages in puff pastry; bowls of scrambled eggs and warming pans holding a variety of omelets. Chelsea spotted a wicker basket heaped with currant scones next to a dish of dark apple butter. She helped herself eagerly, suddenly ravenous. She also selected a slice of ham and a delicate omelet filled with asparagus tips. She waited while Jeff heaped his plate with scones, sausages, and scrambled eggs, and then they returned to their seats.

The table was situated so that they couldn't see any of the other diners, giving Chelsea the sensation that she and Jeff were completely alone. She broke open a scone, buttered it and took a bite. It was even more delicious than she had imagined. She felt Jeff's eyes on her and smiled, nodding appreciatively.

"They're wonderful!"

"What did I tell you?"

She tried to think of something to say to start the conversation. "The view is marvelous." She gestured toward the window and the blue ocean swells beyond. "It makes me want to go down and walk on the beach."

"Good. We'll do that."

She gave him a startled look. "Don't they . . . I mean, do they actually *allow* that?"

"Of course. We're the guests." His penetrating gaze was making her distinctly uncomfortable.

"Well, I was just fantasizing. I really don't have time for that sort of thing."

"It's not a crime to enjoy life, Chelsea. Business isn't the only thing that's important, you know."

Her shoulder blades stiffened. "It is to me."

"Not really. You're just saying that because I make you nervous."

"Nervous? Who said I was nervous?"

"Nobody had to." He smiled and a strand of dark hair fell across his forehead. "It's sticking out all over you. Just relax. I don't bite."

"I am relaxed!" She speared an asparagus tip on her fork, lifted it to her mouth and chewed vigorously.

"Good." He was still giving her that knowing smile.

"Shouldn't we get started on the menu for the party?"

"There's no rush."

"I thought that's why we were here—to work on menu plans over breakfast."

"We have plenty of time."

You might have that luxury, Chelsea thought darkly, but I certainly don't. In my business, there's always more than enough to do to fill every minute of the day. She buttered another scone. It seemed that Jeff had a definite idea of how his role as employer would be executed. And there was little Chelsea could do, short of quitting.

He started talking about sailing, and about the different wind currents and how they affected sailboats. She listened halfheartedly, wondering when in the world he would get around to the party menu. She finished eating first, and waited for him to bring up the subject of the menu. But he still kept talking, going on and on about the fine points of ocean navigation, and she found herself increasingly irritated with his breezy nonchalance. Finally, she could stand it no longer.

"Excuse me, Jeff, but exactly what are your intentions here?"

He gave her a startled frown.

"You brought me here just to . . ." She groped for words. ". . . I don't know what. Just to talk, I guess."

"Is there something wrong with talking?"

"I thought the reason we were here was to discuss the menu. To plan for the surprise party. That's why I brought my notebooks." She felt her cheeks redden under his gaze. "I understood this was to be a business breakfast."

"Ahh, yes. A business breakfast. Well, to tell you the truth, Chelsea, I've never felt that mixing business with pleasure was a very good idea."

"But this isn't pleasure!"

"It isn't?" He leaned back in his chair.

"I didn't mean—" She was suddenly confused. Why was he deliberately misconstruing her words? "The food was wonderful, Seacroft is wonderful, but I thought—"

"Don't." He reached across the table and took her

hand. Little shivers danced up her arm. "Look, I'll be honest with you. I like you. Something happens when I'm with you that I've never experienced before. There's a powerful connection between us."

She felt her palm dampen in his and snatched her hand away. "I don't know what you're talking about."

"Yes, you do."

"No," she said firmly. "I don't."

He pushed back his chair and stood up. "Let's go take that walk on the beach." He didn't wait for her to agree, just came around and held her chair. She was trying to decide if she should just stay put and insist that the waiter bring back her books, when he put his hand on her shoulder. She was suddenly aware that more people had come into the room and several of them were watching her.

She stood up. She knew better than to make a scene in a place like Seacroft. There were people right here, in this very room, who might someday be her clients. She let Jeff take her arm and lead her to a massive oak door. When he opened it, she stepped quickly outside, into the fresh, summer morning.

Chelsea's first step off the stone patio and into the lush green lawn made her high heel sink out of sight. She swayed sideways and Jeff caught her elbow.

"Guess you'd better take off those stilts." Before she could react, he'd squatted in front of her and was slipping off her shoes. His hands felt warm through the sheer mesh of her panty hose. A shiver climbed her spine, and she pushed it away angrily. She was getting tired of the way her body was reacting. This man might be rich and handsome, but he didn't mean anything to her. He was just a client, and there was no reason for the abrupt, electric flutter in her stomach whenever he was near.

He placed her shoes on the edge of the patio, and then, to her surprise, took off his own shoes and socks and rolled the legs of his slacks to mid-calf.

"Come on!" He started down the wide lawn toward the beach. Chelsea followed reluctantly. The scones felt like a weight in the pit of her stomach. She shouldn't be doing this, she knew. She should be poring over her planning books, making notes on the details of the surprise party. She didn't have time for a walk on the beach.

The tide was coming in, tongues of frothy seawater lapping the smooth sand. Chelsea hesitated at the head of the beach and watched Jeff run toward the water. The sand crumbled under his feet, leaving deep, bronze-colored footprints. He ran into the surf, laughing as it splashed up around his legs. He turned and waved her toward him, and when she shook her head, ran back to her. He grabbed her hand and pulled her toward the water.

"No!" she squealed. "I'm not dressed for this!"

But he didn't pay attention, just continued to drag her toward the surf. She felt a wild, reckless excitement build in her as she struggled against his viselike grip. She'd never felt anything like this. It was like being afraid and eager at the same time. It was almost as if she wanted this man to overpower her with his superior strength, to subdue her until she had no will of her own.

"Stop! Please! My panty hose will be ruined!" Her chest was heaving under the tight bodice of her dress, but it wasn't from physical exertion.

"Then take them off." He turned to challenge her with his eyes. His hand still held her wrist tightly.

She shook her head, but it was only a halfhearted shake, and when he gave her another tug toward the water, she pulled away and bent to strip off the wet panty hose. She threw them back onto the beach, where they made a small brown pile that looked like a distant sand castle.

She let him take her hand again, gave it to him, in fact, and they ran together the rest of the way down the sand.

They were standing calf-deep in surf when he kissed her. She was laughing, wet from the hips down, her good black dress dripping saltwater. He turned to her suddenly and took her face in his hands.

It was a pure, bright shock to feel his lips, to discover the intense pleasure of his mouth kneading hers, to taste the salt at the corners of his mouth and the sweet warmth of his tongue. She smelled his breath as it flowed into her, filled her up, left her weak and gasping. She raised her hands instinctively, circling his neck with her arms. He pulled her closer, pressing her body tightly against his; his hands left her face to cradle her back.

When he finally released her, she gazed up at him dizzily. She'd never been kissed that way, had never even *imagined* that a kiss could feel so glorious. It was only when he chuckled that she came to herself.

"Why did you do that?" She tried to muster an indignant tone.

"I think that's pretty obvious."

"Not to me." She backed away from him.

"Oh, I think it was obvious to you too. We've both been anticipating that kiss for the past hour."

She shook her head, took another step backward, and then gasped as a large wave broke behind her, splashing water over her breasts and nearly toppling her into the sea. He was beside her instantly, grasping her around the waist and hauling her toward the shore, but she jerked away from him and ran up onto the beach, aware only of being soaked and humiliated. She searched frantically for her panty hose. She couldn't believe that she'd actually taken them off.

She heard his laugh behind her. " 'After the kiss comes the impulse to throttle.' Come on, Chelsea, relax. We'll go do that planning if you want."

She spun to face him. "The deal's off. I can't work with you."

"What?"

"You heard me. I'm breaking the agreement. Strawberry Lace isn't going to handle your party arrangements."

"You can't do that."

"Sure I can. Just watch me." She spotted her panty hose and started after them, her feet pumping the soft sand like pistons in a hot-wired car.

His hand clamped onto her shoulder. "You signed a contract." His fingers dug into her muscles, forcing her to turn. "You're legally bound."

She gaped up at him for several seconds before she found the right words. "I'm not going to work for you, Jeff Blaine. Not even if you send one of your million-dollar lawyers after me. I'll go to jail first."

His hand dropped away, leaving Chelsea free to march up the slope to the big stone mansion alone. She slipped into her heels and went inside, where she found refuge in the lady's room, which she was relieved to find boasted a pay phone. She put in a call to Lori and asked her to come pick her up right away.

"You're making a big mistake," Lori said. "Not to mention, you're hurting the business."

"Just come," was all Chelsea said.

Chapter Ten

WHEN LORI PULLED UP TO THE SIDE ENtrance of the Seacroft Inn twenty minutes later, Chelsea darted through the glass doors and scrambled into the car.

"Don't ask," she said as Lori frowned at her balled panty hose and wet dress. "Just drive."

Lori obediently sped down the long drive and pulled onto the highway before she started complaining. "You call me up and tell me you need to be picked up, that the Winter deal is off, and I'm supposed to keep my mouth shut? You're going to have to explain exactly what happened."

"It's very simple. I blew it. I misread his signals."

"Whose signals? Blew what? You're not making any sense."

"I'm afraid the surprise party deal is off. I cancelled it."

"You *what?*" Lori gave her a horrified scowl. "You'd better explain exactly what happened, from the beginning."

Chelsea sighed and sagged back in her seat. "Jeff Blaine called me up this morning and said he wanted to discuss the party menu over breakfast at the Seacroft. So, like an idiot, I agreed."

"How does that make you an idiot? It sounds like a wonderful idea."

"He never had any intention of planning the party. He just wanted to add me to his list of conquests."

"Conquests? What on earth are you talking about?"

"He kissed me, that's what I'm talking about."

"Is that a crime?"

"Lori! He's a client, for God's sake!"

"What does that have to do with it?"

"Everything!" Chelsea twisted to face her sister. "It's an employer-employee relationship, Lori. That makes it sexual harassment. Anyway, I'm engaged to Stuart, remember?"

"Only too well." Lori gave her an anxious look. "Are you saying that Jeff attacked you?"

"Not exactly." Chelsea looked out her side window.

"Good. I was beginning to wonder if I'd totally lost my ability to judge character. To tell you the truth, Jeff strikes me as a very sensitive, considerate man. It's very hard for me to imagine him forcing himself on anyone."

"You don't understand."

"No, you're right, I don't. And I think it's a crime to ruin Strawberry Lace's prospects because of one innocent kiss."

"It wasn't innocent!"

"Whatever. I think you'd better find a way to get that job back. Immediately."

Chelsea scowled darkly. "What exactly am I supposed to do? Call Jeff up and apologize? *He* was the one who created the problem!"

"I don't care what you do." Lori's voice was tight. "Just so long as you get the job back."

Chelsea spent the rest of the morning in a white rage. She wanted to smash everything in her apartment, break the china, shred the clothes in her closet with her bare hands, go downstairs and throw Strawberry Lace's pots and pans all around the kitchen. And what made her doubly furious was that Lori was right. She had no right to break the contract just because Jeff had kissed her. When she was honest with herself, she knew it hadn't been sexual harassment at all; she'd wanted that kiss as much as he had. Maybe more. The reason she'd reacted so violently didn't have anything to do with harassment. It had to do with fear, fear of her own feelings, which had been spinning out of control ever since she met him.

She forced herself to sit down with a cup of coffee and try to figure out how to handle the situation. One thing was very, very clear: she couldn't let this kind of thing happen again. For one thing, she was seriously committed to Stuart. She'd promised to marry him, and that certainly meant she couldn't go around kissing other men. For another, she'd seen what happened to Holly. Even if she hadn't been engaged to Stuart, she still couldn't allow herself to respond to Jeff Blaine. She wouldn't risk getting emotionally involved with Muriel Winter's son, no matter how strongly she was attracted to him. Somehow, she had to get her hormones under control and deal with the situation maturely and rationally. She must find a way to get the job back, while making it clear to Jeff that she was unavailable.

She was pouring herself a second cup of coffee

when the idea jumped into her mind. It was so simple she wondered why she hadn't thought of it before. All she had to do was tell Stuart she'd changed her mind about an engagement ring. She'd give him a call and, with what was left of her morning, they could go into Portland to select a ring. Then, in the afternoon, she'd contact Jeff. It would be painful to humble herself and apologize, but it couldn't be helped. Sometimes you had to walk through fire to get where you wanted to go. She'd make sure to mention her engagement, to show him the ring. She knew, from his initial reaction to her reference to Stuart the day they met, that he would be careful to keep his distance.

She was congratulating herself on her ingenuity when the phone rang. Her heart rebelliously skipped a beat when she picked it up and heard Jeff's voice, but she managed to ignore the instant surge of desire that swept through her.

"Chelsea? Are you okay?" He sounded genuinely concerned. "You had me really worried. I couldn't find you."

She took a deep breath. "I'm sorry, Jeff. I know I was rude. I didn't—"

"Save it. It was my fault. I came on too fast and it frightened you. I apologize."

She was at a momentary loss for words. This wasn't the nonchalant, assertive Jeff she recognized. She tried to think what to say next. Get the job back, she reminded herself. That's all that matters. "Jeff, I didn't mean it about breaking the contract. I can't imagine what I was thinking. Strawberry Lace will be happy to cater the party."

There was a long silence. When he spoke, his voice was low. "I've been having second thoughts of my own. I think it would be best to cancel the contract by mutual agreement."

"What? I don't understand."

"I don't think we can develop a working relationship. Things are too volatile between us."

Chelsea felt a cold space open in the center of her body. "I know I was unprofessional, but—"

"It isn't you, Chelsea. It's me."

"I don't understand."

"I think maybe you do," he said quietly. "Look, I have your planning notebooks. I'll drop them by later today. Will you be in?"

"Yes, I have to work on a wedding menu." She could feel tears building at the base of her throat. "Jeff, is there any chance you'll reconsider? Could we at least talk about it?"

"We can always talk." His voice was gentle. "But it would be unfair to encourage you. I think the situation's pretty self-evident."

It occurred to her, as she dropped the phone receiver back into its cradle, that Jeff had just admitted that he was as upset by their relationship as she was. Apparently, the lesson Muriel Winter had taught her youngest son hadn't been lost on her oldest.

She was sitting at the desk in the shop reception room, working out the exact number of racks of lamb for the wedding luncheon, when Jeff came in. He had changed into a pair of jeans and a blue T-shirt and was carrying the notebooks under his arm. He regarded her gravely as he set them on the counter.

"You wanted to talk?"

She ordered her stomach to stop fluttering and smiled up at him. "Yes, thanks for coming. Sit down." She indicated the love seat opposite the desk.

She wished she'd spent some time planning what she was going to say instead of burying her anxiety in menu organization, because he seemed to be waiting for her to open the conversation. She cleared her throat. "I'm hoping we can work things out, Jeff . . ." She paused, tried again. "You see, what happened . . . on the beach . . . was something neither of us wanted . . ."

The trace of a smile touched his mouth. "That's not true."

"Well, it wasn't advisable, under the circumstances."

He nodded.

"And anyway . . ." She balled her fists in her lap, grateful for the bulk of the desk, which hid them from Jeff's penetrating gaze. "Anyway, I promise to try and be a lot more professional in the future."

"Professionalism isn't the problem. I told you that on the phone." He slid forward to brace his forearms on his knees. "The fact is, I'm very strongly attracted to you. And that's not appropriate in a client-buyer relationship."

"But we can be careful. We can just concentrate on the arrangements."

He shook his head. "Whenever I'm with you, any thought of menus or party arrangements just goes right out of my mind. I want to take you places, show you things, make you laugh, kiss you until you can't stand up."

Her eyes widened. She felt a flush climb her cheeks.

"I think the only answer is to cancel the contract, which will leave us free to see each other without any confusing complications."

"See each other? You're saying you want to go out with me?"

"Exactly."

She tried to swallow, but her throat was too dry. Her insides were doing their usual nervous dance at his proximity. "I can't," she said hoarsely.

"Of course you can. We both know that what happened on the beach this morning wasn't accidental. It was inevitable. Frankly, I'm just surprised it didn't happen sooner. The chemistry between us is extraordinary."

She couldn't believe he was saying these things; she'd never heard a man talk so bluntly about his feelings. It aroused her, opened something inside her, made her want to admit that she agreed with him. For a long, vulnerable moment she was even tempted to throw herself into his arms. Instead, she placed her hands on the desk and forced her mouth into a polite smile.

"I'm sorry, but I can't. You see, I'm engaged."

Chelsea saw his grin and realized, with a little shock, that he didn't believe her. It was her own fault, she supposed; she'd used Stuart as an initial barrier between them the first day they met, then recanted her involvement. It had been for the sake of the business then too. But now she had to convince him she was telling the truth. It wasn't just for Strawberry Lace this time, but for her own emotional protection.

"I really am. It happened just a couple of days ago. I haven't got the ring yet."

He straightened his shoulders, slid back into the love seat. "Who's the lucky man?"

"Stuart Potter. You wouldn't know him. He's a local fisherman."

"When's the wedding?"

"We haven't set a date."

"Well. Congratulations." He slapped his palms on his knees and stood up. "I guess I'm the one with egg on my face this time. I apologize for my conduct, both this morning and just now."

"You don't have to apologize. It's my fault. I should have told you sooner."

"Yes, you should have." His eyes were penetrating.

She felt her cheeks flush again in instant, unsettling response. "I'm sorry."

"I'll get over it." He started for the door.

"Wait." She got up and went after him. "This clears things up, doesn't it? There's no reason now that we can't work on the party together."

He turned and frowned down at her. "It seems to me it complicates them. Your engagement doesn't change the chemistry between us; it just makes any further association more explosive. I think it's best if we conclude our business relationship."

"Jeff, please! There must be some way Strawberry Lace can keep the contract! I don't want to beg you, but we really need this job."

He gazed at her a long time before he spoke. "I'll consider it. On the condition that your sister is present at all the meetings."

"My sister? Of course. But she tires easily now; is it really necessary for her to be at all of them?"

"Yes, it is. Because if it's just you and me, the temptation to kiss you again will be too overwhelming to resist." He gave her a breathtaking smile, spun on his heel and left the shop before she could say another word.

* * *

It took Chelsea almost an hour to convince Lori to attend the planning meetings with Jeff Blaine.

"You got Strawberry Lace into this mess," Lori said. "You ought to find a way of getting us out that doesn't involve me. I've got a husband to take care of and a baby on the way. We can't afford the luxury of duplicating our efforts."

"How many times do I have to say I'm sorry? So it's my fault; this is the only way he'll agree to maintain the contract."

Finally, Lori gave in. "Just don't say I never did you any favors, Chels. You owe me a big one."

"I know, I know. I promise to make it up to you. I'll babysit for free every Saturday night when the baby comes."

"Don't think I won't hold you to it. When's our first meeting?"

"As soon as possible. I'll call Jeff right away and get back to you."

She wasn't able to reach Jeff, but she left a message with Beth Harmon and sent up a small prayer that he'd call her back before the day was out. Every hour meant precious time lost that could have been used for party preparation.

She called Stuart and complained for a while about how heavy her schedule was getting. She didn't mention her unsettling encounter with Jeff; the last thing she wanted to do was hurt Stuart. And there was no good reason to tell him; it wasn't as if the kiss really meant anything. She recalled her decision to ask for an engagement ring. "I hope you don't think I'm awful, changing my mind about it," she told him. "The more I thought about it, though, the more I wanted one."

"That's great," he said. "We can go into Portland tomorrow afternoon and pick one out."

"I'll choose something simple, I promise. I know you're strapped for cash right now."

"No problem," Stuart said cheerfully. "And I'm glad you changed your mind. I like the idea of the whole world knowing you belong to me."

"Me too," she said softly.

After she hung up, she worked on the table settings for Saturday's wedding and went over the menu one last time. Things seemed in pretty good order. She'd double-checked the arrangements with the florist and the tent-rental people; verified once again that the bride and groom wanted to use their own table service; the band had been booked for months. As long as the weather cooperated, the reception should come off without a hitch. She was checking her book of price lists when Jeff called.

"I've talked to my sister, and she's agreed to attend all the meetings," Chelsea told him in her best professional tone. "So when would you like the first conference?"

"I'm free tomorrow until noon." His voice sounded remote.

"Would it be convenient for you to come here at ten? Or would you prefer it if we came up to the house?"

"Since it's a surprise party, I think I should come there."

"Fine. I'll have everything ready." For some reason, she didn't want to hang up. "Jeff?"

"Yes?"

"I really am sorry about this morning."

"I'd rather not discuss it further." He hung up

quickly, leaving her holding the receiver in an oddly moist hand.

As she was brushing her teeth that night, Chelsea examined her narrow left hand and tried to imagine what it would look like with an engagement ring on it. The stone would be small, of course, nothing like the huge stone Brandon had given Holly. But it would still be a sign of her commitment to Stuart, her intention to spend the rest of her life with him. Starting this summer. She rinsed out her toothbrush and dropped it into the wall rack. She had to pick a date soon, before her calendar was completely full. There was already so much going on that it was hard to keep everything straight in her mind: the yacht club wedding, the surprise party, the Independence Day affair—if they could manage to change Muriel Winter's mind—the string of weddings through July and August, the tension between herself and Lori, her mother's new boyfriend. Not to mention that morning's extremely disturbing encounter with Jeff. Her own wedding just didn't have any room to squeeze inside her overcrowded brain.

She climbed into bed, flicked off the light, and slid down between the cool sheets. Pictures drifted behind her closed eyelids: the sun on the bright wings of a swooping herring gull, surf licking the beach below the Seacroft Inn, ocean swells breaking over her bare feet. Then an image loomed up that tightened her breath and made the backs of her legs feel suddenly weak: Jeff Blaine taking her face in his hands and kissing her tenderly. She tried to push it away, but it persisted, and when she finally fell asleep, she was being cradled again in Jeff's strong arms, rocked like a child against his broad chest.

* * *

Lori arrived at the shop at nine-thirty the next morning, and together she and Chelsea came up with a tentative menu, so that by the time Jeff came, Chelsea felt reasonably composed. They sat around a small table in the kitchen and Lori ran the meeting. Jeff's dark eyes were directed toward her and avoided Chelsea completely. He agreed quickly to their suggestion of crudités, fruit and cheese, using fresh, seasonal fruits and vegetables and an array of Strawberry Lace's own dips and fondues. There were to be fifteen guests, and the attire would be informal. When Lori brought up the question of the bar, Jeff quickly insisted that he wanted no alcohol served. Chelsea shot him a curious glance at the unusual request. Did it confirm her suspicion that Muriel was an alcoholic? It would make things a bit more demanding for Strawberry Lace the night of the party. Without liquor, a lot of people had trouble loosening up and relaxing.

She left it to Lori to ask all the standard questions about budget, table service, flowers, and the length of the party. Jeff answered matter-of-factly. He didn't even glance at her until the meeting was over and they were standing at the door, politely shaking hands. His eyes locked onto hers for the briefest of moments, then swung away. As he left the shop, a strange, forsaken feeling welled into the pit of her stomach, as if she'd just been informed that someone she loved very much had died.

Chapter Eleven

STUART PICKED CHELSEA UP LATE THAT afternoon, and the first thing he wanted to know was whether she'd picked a wedding date yet.

"No," she sighed, climbing into his battered pickup. "I'm sorry. I honestly haven't had a chance to look at my calendar."

"How about the Fourth of July? It would make it easy to remember our anniversary." He grinned over at her.

"Good idea, except for the little matter of Muriel Winter's party that Strawberry Lace is supposedly putting on that day."

"What do you mean, supposedly?"

"Muriel's having second thoughts. She's talking about calling it off for personal reasons. Frankly, I think the so-called 'personal reason' is that she's drunk all the time. The day I went up there to meet her, she couldn't even walk straight."

Stuart nodded. "I've heard stories. One of the dock workers at the marina saw her fall a few days ago. There's certainly something wrong."

"It serves her right. I've never forgiven her for the way she treated Holly."

"Chels, when it comes to your friends, you're so loyal you wouldn't forgive a fly for landing a yard away."

She laughed. It was always fun being with Stuart. He put things in perspective for her, made her business worries disappear. When she was with him, she felt completely relaxed. There was no unsettling dampening of her palms, no stomach flutters, no startling floods of desire.

Chelsea selected a simple ring, a tiny stone set in a narrow gold band. Stuart made her put it on immediately, then took her to a waterfront restaurant to celebrate. She ordered a seafood salad with vinaigrette dressing and a side order of sugar peas with mushrooms; Stuart ordered steak. She was impressed with the salad when it came; the array of shrimp, scallops, and clams was attractively arranged on a bed of black olives, long strips of sweet red peppers, and julienned scallions. As always, whenever she ate out, she tried to dissect the recipe by analyzing the various flavors. She detected a hint of Dijon mustard and red wine in the dressing, and discovered that the peppers had been roasted. She teased Stuart about ordering such everyday fare when the restaurant's chef obviously had a wonderful flare for gourmet food.

"I'm just trying to make it easy on the chef," he retorted. "When we're married, you're going to be grateful I like simple food best, especially after one of your killer days."

She speared a curl of shrimp and lifted it to her

mouth. "Are you implying that *I'm* going to do all the cooking?"

"Only if you want something edible. You know how I cook. Remember that time I tried to fix you a complete lobster dinner?"

Chelsea laughed. "And boiled lobster's the easiest dinner in the world."

"So they tell me. I guess I've made my point."

"You sure have."

After dinner, Stuart suggested that they go back to his place. "Why don't you spend the night?" he said, leaning over the truck's stick shift and squeezing her knee.

"I wish I could, but I have to get back to the shop. I've got a long evening ahead of me. Next Saturday's yacht club wedding is already giving me a headache." That wasn't true, actually; things were in pretty good shape. But she wasn't entirely comfortable with the thought of sleeping with Stuart.

He put his arm around her. "Your job can wait for once, can't it?" He was gazing at her hopefully. "Please, Chels."

"I'm just so tired." She sighed and let her head rest on his arm. He is your fiancé, an inner voice reminded her. Engaged couples are usually intimate, aren't they? "Okay," she relented. "We'll go to your cabin."

He cupped her cheek with his free hand. "I don't want to push you, if you're not ready."

"You're not, Stuart. Of course I'm ready."

His broad smile told her how much her acquiescence meant to him.

On the way to his house, Stuart chatted about the price of lobster and the upcoming boat races in Boothbay Harbor. He was thinking of going this year, he told her. He could count on her for a copilot, couldn't he?

"It depends on how busy I am," she said. "I'll have to look at my calendar."

"I'm really beginning to resent that calendar, Chels. You're going to have to start penciling me in every day, just so we can talk."

She laughed. "That's not a bad idea."

In his tiny living room, Stuart took her in his arms and kissed her eagerly. She tried to respond by making her hands wander over his chest and back, the way his were roaming over her body. When he unbuttoned her blouse and kissed her breasts, she gasped, but it was less from arousal than surprise. She'd thought of Stuart for so long in terms of friendship that this new intimacy was hard to absorb, even as it was happening. He stroked her neck and back, let his hands slide over her hips and it was then, as he was groping for the button on her skirt, that she pulled away.

"I'm sorry, Stuart," she said, pulling her blouse back over her breasts. "But I'm afraid I'm just too tired. Could we take a rain check? Please?"

She saw the disappointment in his eyes, and felt a strong pang of regret. She reached up to caress his cheek. "I want our first time to be really special," she whispered. "I'd like to be wide awake so I can savor every minute of it."

He sighed and kissed her hand. "You're right. As usual. Come on, I'll take you home."

He kissed her again when he dropped her off. It was a sweet, gentle kiss, but she felt strangely cheated. It's Jeff Blaine's fault, she thought angrily as she climbed the stairs to her apartment. That kiss on the beach spoiled her for anyone else. She froze in mid-climb, appalled at the implication of her thought. Her hand was still trembling a moment later, when she unlocked her door at the top of the stairs.

The next four days were mercifully filled with detailed preparations for the yacht club wedding, so Chelsea didn't have time to think about Stuart or Jeff or anyone but the bridal couple. Saturday dawned sunny, and when she and Lori drove out to the club early that morning to set up, the sky was a shimmering, cloudless blue dome above the van. The reception was scheduled for two, and by noon the decorations were in place and the lawn tent had been set up. Chelsea spent the next hour finishing the cake decoration process, only part of which could be done in the shop. She used a fluted pattern for the frosting, and added real white roses to the icing rosettes she'd constructed around the cake's sharp edges. She topped it off with a spray of fragrant roses, baby's breath, and lemon leaves. Then she and Lori carried it into the dining room and placed it in the center of the long buffet table in front of the fireplace.

By 1:45 everything was ready. The waiters had arrived and both Chelsea and Lori had changed into their Strawberry Lace uniforms. The trademark basket of strawberries was positioned unobtrusively near the door to the kitchen, and the bartender had already uncorked the champagne.

The guests started to drift in just before two. Lori was busy in the kitchen, spreading chicken paté on heart toasts, while Chelsea was making last minute adjustments to the display of crystal champagne glasses on the long bar. As the first guest entered, she nodded to the waiters to start pouring champagne, then slipped over to a side window, to keep an eye out for the bride and groom.

But what she saw, as she gazed out at the parking lot, made her breath lock in her throat. There, only a few feet beyond the window, emerging from a long, gray Cadillac, was the familiar figure of Muriel Winter, followed by Jeff Blaine.

Lori glanced up from the silver tray where she was arranging toast hearts as Chelsea burst into the kitchen.

"What happened? You look like you've seen a ghost."

"It's Jeff Blaine! He and his mother are guests at the wedding."

"So? This *is* the society wedding of the season, you know." Lori's pretty face crinkled into a smile. "Why are you blushing like that?"

"Am I?" Chelsea pressed her hands to her cheeks.

"Most definitely. And it's a very charming effect too. Goes with your hair." Lori placed the tray next to a platter of glistening white coconut serviche. "It's Jeff, isn't it? You've got a crush on him."

"I have no such thing!"

"I recognize an infatuation when I see one, Chels. I'm just surprised I didn't pick up on it earlier. Must be my reflexes are slowing down because of Junior, here." She patted her belly affectionately.

"You couldn't be more wrong. I'm engaged, remember?"

"How convenient. Good old Stuart protects you once again from the predatory American male. One of these days Stuart is going to realize what's really going on and he's going to be deeply hurt. Have you thought of that?"

"I'd never do anything to hurt Stuart!"

Lori's smile disappeared. "Then maybe you should break the engagement, before he starts believing you're in love with him."

"I *am* in love with him!"

"No, you're not. And you never will be. Stuart's just not the right kind of man for you."

"I don't know why you keep saying that!" Chelsea's eyes stung. "Stuart's the *perfect* man for me! He's the most wonderful, good-natured, hardworking man in the world! It would take a hundred idle, rich playboys like Jeff Blaine to fill his shoes! You have no right to tear him apart this way!"

Lori put a comforting arm around her shoulder. "I'm not tearing him apart. I like Stuart too. And I know he'll make someone a wonderful husband. But not you, Chels. You need somebody a lot stronger, a lot more masterful."

"Masterful? You sound like you've been reading too many Gothic romances." Chelsea jerked away angrily. "I don't need any advice from you, big sister. I can handle my own life." She snatched a paper towel from the roll and wiped her eyes. "Where are the waiters? We should start serving the hors d'oeuvres."

The wedding reception went smoothly. The tiny ham and cheese croissants were a big hit; the bridal cake was described by several guests as stunning; the salmon gravlax was the most delicate the bride's mother had ever tasted. By the time the dancing began, the waiters were already circulating with their fourth round of Roquefort grapes. Lori took a break and went to rest on the couch in the little sitting room off the kitchen. Chelsea was setting out another platter of chocolate petits fours when one of the waiters hurried into the kitchen.

"They're calling for the chef," he told Chelsea. "The bridal couple wants to toast you." He grabbed Chelsea's arm and pulled her through the swinging door into the dining room.

"To the chef!" cried the groom from the far end of the room, where the dance floor had been established. He lifted a wineglass toward Chelsea. The music stopped and everyone in the room turned to face her. The applause was deafening.

She caught a glimpse of Jeff, standing in back of the groom and she knew she was blushing even before he smiled at her. She bowed and tried to slip quickly back into the safety of the kitchen, but the groom's voice stopped her. "Let's have a dance in her honor." He turned to the band leader. "A waltz, please."

The leader nodded. Chelsea saw the groom take the bride's hand and tilt his head briefly to speak to Jeff. Then she watched with growing alarm as Jeff crossed the floor to her.

"May I have this dance?" He bowed and held out his arm. "At the groom's request."

She couldn't do anything but accept, not with so many people watching. As Jeff led her onto the dance floor, Chelsea experienced such a violent trembling in the base of her spine that she was afraid her knees would buckle. Jeff swept her gracefully into his arms the instant before she collapsed. And suddenly she was in paradise.

She'd never experienced anything like it. She'd danced before; she loved to dance; she and Stuart often went dancing in Portland on Saturday nights.

Though Stuart wasn't an expert, he was a competent dancer, and she'd always liked the harmonious movement of their bodies in time to music. But it was nothing like this.

This was magic; this was bliss; this was pure, unadulterated ecstasy. She felt as if she were soaring, floating above the floor in Jeff's strong arms. The music was in her and around her simultaneously; she was one with it. All the panic and anger and anxiety of the past few days vanished completely. She closed her eyes and leaned her head lightly against his broad shoulder. She felt his arm tighten around her in response and, in one tiny part of her brain, knew she'd made a mistake, that she shouldn't have moved closer to him, but she couldn't help it. She wasn't in control anymore; she was *being* controlled. By the amazing, masterful dancing of Jeff Blaine.

She didn't even realize the waltz had ended until he gently pulled away from her.

"Oh." She took a step backward and felt suddenly dizzy. When she glanced up at him, she saw that he was gazing at her. Their eyes locked and the dizzy sensation increased. She was vaguely aware that another waltz had begun, but she couldn't pull her eyes away from Jeff's. She took another step backward, bumped into someone and stumbled on the heel of her left pump. She reached for Jeff to steady herself. It was an involuntary, reflex action, but when she straightened and started to turn away, he didn't release her hand.

"Another dance?" Without waiting for her answer, he pulled her into his arms. Again she was instantly transported, aware only of the warmth of his hard body pressing against hers, the scent of his cologne in her nostrils, the pressure of his hand on her back.

When the dance ended, he led her back to the kitchen door.

She looked up at him and tried to smile. "Thanks."

"Thank *you.*" He took a strawberry from the basket beside the door and bit into it. For some reason, she couldn't take her eyes off him. She watched the tip of his tongue emerge and lick away a smear of strawberry juice from his lower lip. Then, without averting his gaze, he picked up another strawberry and lifted it to her mouth.

Her lips opened automatically to receive the fruit. It wasn't until she bit into the sweet, red flesh that she grasped the sexual overtones of his gesture. She glanced up at him again, saw the same knowledge reflected in his eyes, and spit the remains of the strawberry into her hand.

Her cheeks blazed. "I have to get back to work," she croaked, and fled into the kitchen.

She was standing at the sink, furiously scrubbing a cake pan, when the kitchen door swung open a few minutes later. For a heart-stopping moment she was afraid that Jeff had followed her into the kitchen, but when she looked up, she saw it wasn't Jeff, but his mother.

Chelsea dropped her pan back into the dishwater. "Can I help you, Mrs. Winter?" She tried to make her voice sound even and controlled. "Are you looking for someone?"

"Yes," came the answer, in the same icy tone Chelsea remembered from her other brief encounters. "I'm looking for you."

Chelsea dried her hands on a towel hanging over the sink. "What can I do for you?"

Muriel took a step into the kitchen, swayed, and caught the edge of the counter to steady herself. Chelsea pulled one of the kitchen's tall stools over to the older woman. "Is something wrong with the food?"

Muriel frowned and imperiously waved away the stool. "The food is fine. Wonderful, in fact. This has nothing to do with food." She tried to straighten her shoulders, but her right arm still clutched the counter for balance.

Chelsea kept her smile pasted on, hoping that it might soften Muriel's glare, while she waited for the woman to speak. She was obviously furious about something; Muriel's intense blue eyes looked like they were trying to bore a hole through her skull.

"It's about my son," Muriel said. "I saw Jefferson dance with you."

"Yes. It was at the request of the groom."

"I realize that." She groped for a stronger purchase on the counter edge. "But I saw the way he looked at you. I want to make something plain to you, Miss Adams. My son is not available to you, or to anyone in your social station. Is that clear?"

Chelsea stared at her. The woman had incredible audacity. And apparently a vivid imagination to go along with it. She straightened her shoulders. "I'm not interested in your son, Mrs. Winter. Except as a client."

Muriel raised a skeptical eyebrow. "I'm not a stupid woman, Miss Adams. I saw the looks that passed between you."

"I'm afraid you were mistaken. It may interest you to know, Mrs. Winter, that I've recently become engaged. I guarantee there's nothing between me and Jeff."

"As long as you understand my meaning, Miss Adams. If Jefferson were to become romantically involved with you, the consequences to your catering business would be devastating, I can assure you." She swayed forward; Chelsea wasn't certain if the movement was deliberate or not, but it was distinctly menacing.

"Thank you for your warning." Chelsea's own voice was icy. "If there's nothing else you wish to discuss, I'll get back to my work."

"One more thing." Muriel raised a bony index finger. "I want you to know that my cancellation of the Independence Day affair had nothing to do with the competence of Strawberry Lace. As long as you heed my warning, I will consider recommending you to my friends. The hors d'oeuvres today were delicious."

"I'm glad you enjoyed them."

Muriel turned to leave, and Chelsea hurried back to the sink. She had to push her hands down into the warm, soapy water and hold them there for a long time before they stopped shaking.

Chapter Twelve

CHELSEA WAS SEETHING AS SHE FINISHED washing the cake pans and slammed them into their box. She felt as if she'd just been clubbed. Muriel clearly hadn't believed her when she said she had no interest in Jeff. The woman was unwilling to let go of her two adult sons, and paranoid of any woman who came within two feet of them. There was only one word for a woman like Muriel, and it was a word Chelsea rarely used, but it fit so perfectly in this case that she said it aloud as she rinsed silverware under hot water.

She had planned to tell Lori about Muriel's intimidating warning, but when she saw the exhaustion on her sister's face as she came out of the sitting room, she decided against it. Lori's cheeks were pale, her eyes puffy with fatigue, and she looked like she could easily sleep for a week.

"Why don't you go home, sis? I can handle the clean-up. I'll grab a couple of waiters, pay them overtime."

"We can't afford that." Lori shook her head and

picked up a stack of empty trays. "Besides, I promised I'd do my share until the baby comes."

"That was before you knew how much pregnancy takes out of you. I don't want you pushing yourself. It's not good for you, and I'm sure it's not good for the baby."

Lori sighed. "Maybe you're right. It seems like I'm tired all the time lately. Are you sure you don't mind if I take off?"

"It was my idea," Chelsea reminded her. "Now go before I get nasty." She gave her a mock scowl.

"Thanks a million. I owe you."

"Just consider it as payment for sitting in on the arrangements with Jeff."

"I'll do that." Lori pulled on her sweater and slipped out the back door.

Chelsea felt a wave of satisfying warmth. It was good to be the giver for a change. Usually Lori was the generous one, so quick to help, charitable to a fault. She'd give you the shirt off her back. It was about time she did a little receiving.

She spoke to two of the waiters, who agreed to help with the clean-up at the regular rate. After all the guests left, the three of them washed dishes, took apart the elaborate bridal decorations, collected the flowers for distribution to area nursing homes, and oversaw the disassembly of the tent. Chelsea sublimated her raging anger at Muriel Winter into her work and they finished earlier than she expected. By nine-thirty she was driving back to her apartment to unload the van. But her furious pace had taken more out of her than she realized. By the time everything was put away and both the shop and van were locked up, she was almost stumbling with fatigue.

She took off her heels and climbed the stairs to her

apartment, her left hand holding the shoes, her right stuck deep in her purse, searching for her key. At the top, she stopped to peer into the dark vinyl bag. She didn't see the white, rectangular box in front of her door until she stepped on it. She lost her balance and almost fell, only saving herself by grabbing the railing. Her shoes fell down the stairs with a clatter.

"Damn!" Why would anyone leave a box at the top of the stairs? The mailman always slid her mail into the wide slot in the door at the bottom of the stairs. The box wasn't too big for that. It looked like a clothing gift box. She bent and picked it up. There was no name on it, no address. She could only assume that someone had placed it at her door by accident, thinking it was someone else's apartment.

She retrieved her heels, found her key, and let herself in. She picked up the crushed package and took it into the kitchen, flicked on the light and turned the box over. A small card was taped onto the bottom. Her name was written on it in handsomely slanted script.

She detached the card and stared down at it. She didn't recognize the handwriting. It obviously wasn't from anybody she knew, but it was definitely for her. She opened it slowly, a strange feeling of dread filling her chest.

It was a thank-you card. On the cover, a wash of rainbow watercolors was the background for the words *thank you* in casual black calligraphy. Inside, a short note in the same attractive penmanship read: *I know you can put this to good use. Thanks for the dance.*

It was from Jeff. It had to be. Who else had she danced with besides Stuart in the past five years?

She dropped the card onto the table. Her hands were shaking as she opened the box, which was sealed with short strips of tape. She lifted the cover, unfolded a blanket of white tissue paper and gasped in surprise.

She touched the teal-blue velour with trembling fingers. It was the bathrobe she had admired at the mall three weeks ago. The seventy-dollar bathrobe! She lifted it out and held it up in front of her. It was gorgeous, more beautiful than she'd remembered. It had a long zipper and a lime-green satin ribbon that tied at the neck. The sleeve cuffs were banded in matching satin. She closed her eyes and pinched herself, to make sure she wasn't dreaming, but when she opened them again, she was still holding the robe.

She spotted the card and flushed as she remembered her embarrassment when Jeff had caught her wearing her father's old bathrobe. But how had he known this was the robe she wanted? And more important, what was his motivation for giving it to her?

She placed the robe back in its box and gazed down at it. Her mind somersaulted back to what she had been deliberately avoiding all evening: the dance. She had a sudden, vivid memory of herself in Jeff's arms, spinning to the sweet rhythm of the waltz. She'd never taken drugs, but she imagined that they must feel something like what she had felt then. Just remembering it opened a deep yearning inside her. She wanted to experience the dance again; she wanted to be in Jeff's arms again. Forever.

She abruptly cut off her thoughts. This was ridiculous. It was her fatigue talking, nothing more. She loved Stuart.

She folded the robe and placed it back inside its box. She couldn't keep it, that was clear. In the morning she would call Jeff and tell him she appreciated the thought, but couldn't accept the bathrobe.

And she would remind him again that she was engaged.

She remembered the meeting with Jeff and Lori even before she saw it on her calendar the next morning. She wondered why it had slipped her mind last night. It was the perfect opportunity to return the bathrobe to Jeff.

She dressed in a knit blouse and green cotton jumper and was waiting in the shop when Lori drove up. The first thing Lori did when she entered the shop was point to the box sitting on the display counter.

"What's that?"

"A mistake." Chelsea looked up from the itemized bill she was writing at the desk. "Go ahead, take a look, if you want."

Lori lifted the cover of the box. "It's beautiful! And it's in your color."

"Yes, I've had my eye on that robe for weeks."

"Then what do you mean, a mistake?"

"It's not mine." Chelsea stacked the invoice sheets in a neat pile and stood up. "It belongs to Jeff."

Lori laughed. "Don't be silly. It's a woman's robe." Her eyes widened as she comprehended Chelsea's meaning. "You mean he gave it to you?"

Chelsea nodded.

"What's the occasion?"

"There isn't any. It was waiting for me when I got home last night. He must have gone to the mall and bought it after the reception."

Lori's grin broadened. "Looks like you've hooked a rather impressive fish, Chels. Congratulations."

"I haven't hooked anything!" Chelsea reached over and jammed the cover back down onto the box.

"I'm giving it back to him when he comes this morning."

"You're kidding! It's gorgeous!"

"I can't accept a gift like that. We're not just talking a box of chocolates, you know. That robe cost seventy dollars!"

"I think you're making too much out of this. It's just a bathrobe. For a man like Jeff Blaine, seventy dollars is pocket change."

Chelsea set her jaw. "I'm giving it back anyway."

"I don't understand why you're making such a big deal. It's not a diamond necklace or anything. But I guess you have to do what you have to do."

"That's right. I don't want Stuart to be jealous."

Lori laughed. "Stuart doesn't have a jealous bone in his body, and you know it."

"Our relationship's changed, Lori. I told you that."

"Whatever you say. Well, get ready. Here comes Mr. Handsome now."

Chelsea's stomach lurched violently as the shop door chimed open and Jeff walked in. It was all she could do to pick up the box.

"I see you got the robe." He was smiling, that same breathtaking smile he'd worn when she first met him.

"Jeff, I can't . . ." She clutched the box in both hands. "You have to return it."

"What's the matter? Doesn't it fit?"

"Yes, but I . . . can't accept it." She felt so stupid, standing there under his dark gaze, fumbling for words. It wasn't like her to be tongue-tied.

"Why not? You needed a new bathrobe. I had a few extra bucks. What's the problem?"

"It's just not appropriate. I mean . . . I'm engaged." She was intensely aware of Lori's amusement. Her sister was doing everything she could to keep from laughing.

"So, it's an engagement present." Abruptly, he reached over and covered her hand with his, right there on the box. "Keep it, with my congratulations."

She glanced quickly at Lori, who was giving her a look that said, *What did I tell you?* She sighed and gave up. Her sister was right. What was the harm in keeping a bathrobe that in Jeff's eyes probably involved about as much financial sacrifice as a pack of chewing gum did for her? He had acknowledged her engagement. It didn't appear that he was using the gift to try to woo her away from Stuart. She took a deep breath and smiled at him. "Well, thank you. It's lovely."

"I thought so."

Lori sat down on the love seat. "I'm curious how you picked it, Jeff. Did you know that Chelsea's had her eye on this particular robe?"

He shook his head. "It just looked like something she should have." His dark eyes slid toward Chelsea and he smiled.

"Well, let's get down to business," Chelsea said quickly. "We have a lot of work to do."

She was distinctly uncomfortable through the whole meeting, even though it ran as smoothly as the last. It wasn't just that she still felt confused about the gift, or about Lori's reaction to it. It was the fact that Jeff's gaze rarely left her face, although Lori did most of the talking. He would glance only briefly at the papers set in front of him, then his eyes would settle again on her, as if drawn there by a powerful magnet. She felt her cheeks growing pinker and pinker as time passed, until she was sure they were flaming crimson.

She was surprised when, after Jeff left, Lori didn't admit to being aware of the fact that he'd been watching her.

"How could you have missed it? He was staring at me the whole time!"

"I think your imagination's running away with you, Chels." Lori smiled, the condescending, big-sister smile that Chelsea had always hated. Then she delivered her coup de grace. "Anyway, how did you know he was looking at you all the time, unless you were looking at him?"

Chelsea felt exhausted after the one-hour meeting, as if she'd just been through a marathon planning session with a big Portland hotel. After Lori left, instead of getting to work on filling out orders, she drifted around the shop for a while. She checked the whereabouts of the various utensils they'd need for party preparation, and then decided to take the afternoon off. She deserved a break after yesterday's wedding. And she needed to get away, go where she didn't recognize any faces, where no one would recognize her.

The weather was cool and sunny, a good day for hiking. An hour later, dressed in her cut-off jeans and I LOVE MAINE T-shirt, she headed up the coast to the bird sanctuary. It was a wonderful place to walk, and not many people frequented it. She wasn't much of a bird watcher, but she did like seeing the ospreys and cormorants in the tidal marshes.

The tide was coming in, bringing the water close to the edges of the path in some places. A light breeze bent the tops of the tall marsh grass, while small birds swooped and dived into its thick, silver-green shelter. As she walked, Chelsea felt her tension melting away. Lori, she realized, had been right about the robe. It was no big deal, especially not to a man like Jeff Blaine. The rich, she knew, lived unconventionally, had unusual values. Money separated you, made you different. She sighed. She wouldn't mind being rich herself. The constant struggle to make ends meet wore her down. But things were starting to look up. Once Muriel Winter started recommending Strawberry Lace to her friends—*if* she did—their troubles would be over.

She was walking down a steep trail between thick beds of marsh grass when she slipped on a patch of mud. She felt her left knee strike something hard as she went down, but the only pain she noticed was the sharp jolt in her right wrist as her outstretched hands smashed heavily to the ground. She hauled herself back to her feet and examined her wrist. It was already swelling. She sighed, berating herself for her clumsiness; she had no choice but to abandon the hike and go home. The sooner she packed it in ice, the better. With a little luck, the swelling would go down and the injury wouldn't hamper her work. She started back along the trail, and realized immediately that she'd injured her knee as well.

The pain wasn't much more than a dull ache, but the joint was stiff and awkward. She took a deep breath and forced down the alarm that rose in her. It wouldn't do any good to panic; it would just slow her down. At the rate she was going, it would take her a good hour to get back to the car. She headed up the path, doggedly limping along, doing what she could to take the stress off her knee. She was entering a long stretch of woods when she heard the voices. She couldn't see the source, but it sounded like a man and woman. A few minutes later, in the dimly lit distance of the shaded trees, two figures emerged from the far side of a boulder.

A sudden thump in her chest made Chelsea catch her breath. Even at this distance and in the shadowy light, she recognized Jeff Blaine and Beth Harmon.

"Hey!" She waved her arms eagerly. "Over here! I need help!"

Jeff came running. "What's wrong?"

"It's my knee. I fell and hurt it somehow."

He squatted in front of her, probing her knee with gentle fingers. She winced as a sharp pain jolted her leg.

"Can you walk?"

"Yes, sort of."

He stood up. "Show me."

She took a few lopsided steps along the path, aware of his intense scrutiny.

"It looks like it's uncomfortable, but not unstable. You're obviously able to put some weight on it."

She nodded.

He bent again to run his fingers along the inside of her knee. "I think you've probably pulled the medial tarsal ligament."

"Medial tar—what?"

He ignored her question and straightened, frowning. "You must have taken quite a tumble. Does anything else hurt?"

"Just my wrist." She held out her arm. He cradled her wrist in his left hand while he examined it with his right.

He whistled softly. "I don't think this is your lucky day, Chelsea. This is a pretty bad sprain."

"I was afraid of that."

"We need to get both of them packed in ice as quickly as possible." He turned to Beth, who was dressed in khaki slacks and a knit blouse, her attractive face lined with concern. "Looks like you and I are going to have to serve as crutches today. Are you up to it?"

Beth nodded.

"I can walk," Chelsea protested.

"Not if you have any intention of recovering quickly," Jeff said curtly. He and Beth quickly linked arms around Chelsea's back and they started along the path.

It took over thirty minutes to reach the parking lot, and by then Chelsea's shoulders ached from the uncomfortable position. She slid away from them and hobbled to her Toyota, where she opened the door and sank into the driver's seat with a sigh. She closed her eyes for a minute, and when she opened them, Jeff was standing over her, frowning.

"You can't drive in that condition."

"Sure I can."

He shook his head. "You're a safety hazard. Slide over. I'm taking you home." He handed Beth the keys to his car and leaned in to nudge Chelsea out of the seat. "Come on. Over."

She was too tired and in too much discomfort to argue. She shifted awkwardly into the passenger seat and watched Jeff climb behind the wheel. He started the car, jerked it into gear, and headed out of the parking lot.

"I'm sorry for putting you out," she said once they were on the highway. "I guess I ruined your date."

"Date?"

"With Beth. I'm really sorry."

"Oh." He laughed. "Well, it's not really what you'd call a date. Beth and I are just good friends."

"Oh." Chelsea blinked. "Well, they say a good friendship is a solid basis for romance."

"Do they? Funny, I've never heard that. Beth and I enjoy each other's company, but there's not"—He frowned, searching for the right word—"well, our relationship is missing that special chemistry you need for romance." He glanced at her, and she felt a shiver of alarm at his expression. As if he were telling her something very intimate with his eyes.

She averted her head quickly to stare out at the roadside flying past.

Chapter Thirteen

AT HER APARTMENT, JEFF HELPED CHELsea up the stairs and settled her onto the couch. He made her stretch out with her knee propped on a pillow while he located the two ice packs in her freezer and tied them around her injured joints with long strips of gauze.

"I know it hurts," he said, "but I want you to leave them on for ten minutes. Then I'll wrap your wrist and knee for support. Do you have a couple of Ace bandages?"

She shook her head.

"Then I'll use gauze temporarily. I'll get some bandages to you before the day's out."

"I can buy my own."

"There's no need. I've got half a dozen in my car. I'll give Beth a call, have her run them down to me."

Chelsea frowned as he picked up the phone, dialed quickly and spoke in a low voice into the receiver. Why on earth would he carry a bunch of Ace bandages around in his car? Wasn't that a little overcautious? Was the man some kind of fitness freak?

He hung up. "She can't get away for a couple of

hours. So I'm afraid I'm stuck here. Unless you'd like me to call a taxi."

"No, stay. Please."

He came back to the couch and squatted beside her, slid one finger gently under the ice pack and palpated her swollen knee. "I'm pretty sure you've only stretched the ligaments on the inside of your leg. But it wouldn't hurt to get an X ray."

"No! I'll be all right, I'm sure."

He looked at her. "What is it with you and hospitals anyway? Do they frighten you that much?"

She shook her head. "It's something you wouldn't understand."

"Try me."

Something softened inside her at his worried look. "It's money," she confessed. "I don't have any health insurance and I can't afford an X ray right now." She felt the heat of embarrassment rise in her cheeks.

"I'm sorry. I didn't realize. Look, I'd be happy to pay for it."

"No! Absolutely not!" She was instantly sorry when his eyes darkened at the rebuff. "At least not unless it doesn't get better on its own in a couple of days," she amended.

"All right. That's fair enough. But you're going to have to stay off it for at least forty-eight hours. I'll get you a set of crutches so you can manage things around the apartment. But don't try the stairs."

"I can't stay up here that long! I have work to do in the shop!"

He straightened. "It can't be helped. If you want the sprains to heal, you have to give your joints a chance to rest." He pulled a chair over to the couch next to her and sat down. "Can't your sister take up the slack for a couple of days?"

Chelsea shook her head. "She's already working too hard. She was so tired last night, she had to leave the reception before it was over."

He nodded. "You're right. She needs to take care of herself at this stage of her pregnancy. She's about eight months along, isn't she?"

"Yes, how did you know?"

"Experience."

Chelsea's eyes widened. "You have children?"

He laughed. "No, I'm a physician."

"A *physician?* But I thought—"

"You thought I was rich and idle."

She blushed. "Not exactly. I just assumed you were like Brandon—working on investment portfolios, taking long vacations in foreign countries, that sort of thing. You told me you were in Africa last year. . . ." Her voice drained away at the sight of his widening grin.

"I was. For the last two years, as a matter of fact. I'm a doctor with Project HOPE."

"What's that?"

"A nonprofit organization that trains and educates local health-care workers all over the world. We teach them to assume responsibility for their country's own health delivery systems. There's an enormous need for that in Africa, where AIDS is epidemic."

She stared at him. "I had no idea you were a doctor."

"Well, actually I'm more of a teacher. At least when I'm working overseas."

"So why did you come back?"

"Family reasons." A shadow of pain flickered across his eyes.

She could tell that he didn't want to discuss it, but she somehow sensed it was his mother he was talking about. "I'm sorry. Are you planning on going back to Africa eventually?"

"I don't know." He shifted in his chair and directed his gaze out the window. "I'll just have to wait and see what develops."

Jeff fixed a simple supper of tomato soup and peanut butter sandwiches, and brought it to Chelsea on a tray. The throbbing in her wrist had diminished and she was feeling reasonably comfortable. She was surprised at how easy it was to talk to him. Despite the occasional erotic flutter in her stomach and chest, she was able to relax. They talked about a host of different things: everything from sailing to politics. She found herself opening up to him in a way she rarely did with men other than Stuart. Something in Jeff made her relax at the very center of her being; it was as if his compassion and intelligence stimulated her own. They were soon laughing over the local town council's latest antics.

The discovery that Jeff was a doctor had a strange effect on Chelsea. It made him seem more likable, more human somehow. He obviously wasn't in it for the money; with his credentials, he could easily have set up a lucrative practice in a wealthy Boston suburb. Instead, he'd chosen to work among the poorest of the poor, turning his back on the pampered world of Muriel Winter.

When the phone rang just after seven, she felt it as an irritating intrusion. Jeff picked it up before she could reach it. He spoke briefly and handed it to her.

"Your fiancé."

Chelsea took the phone. "Stuart?" She watched as Jeff withdrew to the kitchen, but even so, she was uncomfortably aware of his presence in the apartment as she spoke.

"Who's the dude?" Stuart's tone was a mixture of cheerfulness and curiosity.

"My doctor," she said quickly. "I went hiking and sprained my knee and he happened along."

"Are you okay? Would you like me to come over?"

"No, I'm fine. Or I will be in a couple of days." She related the details of her accident.

"I wondered what happened to you. I tried to call you at the shop earlier. I thought you were going to be working all afternoon."

"It was a spur of the moment thing."

"Are you sure you don't want me to come?"

"I'm sure."

"Call me if you change your mind. I love you, Chels."

"I love you too," she said softly.

The minute she hung up, the phone rang again. It was Beth Harmon for Jeff. He spoke only briefly before he dropped the receiver into its cradle.

"She won't be able to pick me up until ten at the earliest," he informed Chelsea. "I told her to forget it. Mother's having a bad day, and I don't want her left alone."

Chelsea nodded. "Why don't you take my car? It doesn't look like I'll be needing it."

"Thanks, but a taxi will be fine." But instead of calling one, he sat down again and shifted his chair even closer to the couch. A moment later he had picked up their conversation where they left off, detailing a funny, socially-complicated circumstance he'd been involved in while teaching at a hospital in Zimbabwe.

Chelsea listened with fascination, instantly caught up again in the story, and by the time she looked at the clock, it was almost eleven. He saw her glance.

"I'm afraid I'm keeping you up." He got to his feet.

"No, I enjoyed it. Really. Your stories are riveting." Suddenly, she didn't want him to leave. She wanted to go on listening to his resonant voice for hours.

"Thanks, but I think I'd better get you to bed."

"I can manage." She sat up and started to swing her legs to the floor, but his arm stopped her.

"No you don't. This isn't the right time to be reckless." To her surprise, he bent and quickly lifted her into his arms. She was intensely aware of the heat of his body as he carried her into the bedroom and placed her gently on the bed. Then he went to her closet and pulled out the robe he'd given her. "Here, put this on."

"Now?"

He nodded. "You're going to need some help getting those shorts off over the swelling."

She propped herself against the headboard as she struggled to slip into the bathrobe. But even with its abundant folds concealing most of her body, she felt acutely aware of Jeff's proximity as she reached under the robe and tugged her shorts down to her knees.

"This may hurt a little," he said as he squatted in front of her and started to gently ease the tight denim over her swollen knee. She saw at once that he was right; it wasn't something she could have done easily on her own. Despite her flexibility, it would have been impossible to manage this smooth, sliding motion by herself.

It took much longer than she expected, but finally the shorts were off. She tried to make her heart slow down. The sensation of his fingers on the bare skin of her legs had shocked her, leaving her whole body tingling with excitement. He palpated the swelling once again and settled her leg very gently on the bed.

Despite the throbbing pain, Chelsea wanted him to touch her again. Not just her knee and wrist, but her whole body. She wanted to feel his fingers flow across her skin, caressing her tenderly. She caught his hand as he straightened.

"Don't go yet."

He frowned. "Is it the pain? Is it worse?"

"No. I . . ." She released his hand. "It's nothing. Thanks for your help."

But he had read her desire somehow, in that instant between his question and the separation of their hands. He sat beside her on the bed and, very slowly, without saying a word, slipped his right hand under the hair at the back of her neck and brought her face toward his.

Her lips felt engorged, eager for his kiss, and when his mouth finally descended on hers, she gave a tiny moan of joy. His lips massaged hers and his tongue traced the tender membrane inside her mouth. He drew her closer, cradling her against him firmly. Then he was lowering himself onto the bed and stretching out beside her. She realized, with only a flicker of alarm, that she was on the verge of surrendering to him, that soon he could do anything with her that he wished. She had never felt this way before in her life, had never even imagined feeling such intense yearning. This is what they mean when they say making love, she thought. It isn't just a euphemism for sex; it's something entirely different. She felt his hand cup her breast outside the robe as his mouth moved from her lips to her neck. She moaned again and pressed herself against him.

Suddenly, he released her and sat up. It was such an abrupt, unexpected movement, that Chelsea gasped. And then she was flooded with a horrible, drenching sense of loss as he shook his head and raked his hand through his hair.

"I'm sorry," he said tightly. "That was inexcusable." He stood up quickly. "I'll call a taxi and let myself out."

He left the room before she could say anything, and moments later she heard the front door open and close, followed by the muted sound of his feet going down the stairs to the street.

Chelsea slept fitfully that night, and in the morning she called Lori to explain why she couldn't meet her at the fish market in Portland as they'd planned.

"Don't worry," Lori reassured her. "I'll take care of everything. Paul's free today; he can give me a hand. You just rest and get well."

"If you could get the materials to me, I can work on place settings."

"Sure, no problem. So Jeff Blaine had to rescue you again? This is starting to sound redundant, Chels."

Chelsea groaned. "I know! It seems like whenever I do something that makes me feel like a total idiot, he's there to notice. Just my luck!"

"Maybe it's not luck. Maybe it's karma. Maybe you and Jeff are being drawn together for a reason."

"Lori, cut it out! How many times do I have to point out to you that I'm getting married to Stuart?"

"Maybe until you convince me you're in love with him."

"I *am* in love with him!"

"You're leaning on him like a crutch, Chelsea. You're using him to avoid taking risks. That's what you've done from the very beginning."

"Look, I didn't propose to him! He was the one who wanted to get married."

"Of course he did. I never said *he* wasn't in love with *you*. You're the one who's not playing fair. Cut him loose, Chelsea. The longer you let things go on this way, the more hurt he's going to be when he realizes the truth."

"I can't believe you're saying these horrible things!"

"There's nothing horrible about suggesting you should be honest with him. And yourself."

Tears stung the corners of Chelsea's eyes. She took a deep breath to steady her voice. "You don't understand the first thing about my relationship with Stuart! Maybe if you weren't so determined to tell me how to live my life, you'd see how good we are for each other."

"I'm sorry." Lori's tone was instantly contrite. "I know you have to live your own life. It's just that I don't want you to miss out on the best part. I love you too much. Think about what I said. Okay?"

"Okay." Chelsea hung up, feeling strangely depleted. Maybe it was her lack of sleep. Or the pain in her knee. Or maybe it was because Lori's advice had hit much too close to home.

* * *

Stuart called in mid-morning offering to help in the shop.

"Oh thanks." She laughed. "It isn't enough that I'm injured; you want to ruin Strawberry Lace's reputation too. We both know what the paté would taste like if you mixed it. Besides, don't you have to haul today?"

"Yeah, but I don't like the idea of being out on the water while you're lying in bed, racked with pain."

She laughed again. "I'm not racked with pain, Stuart. Honestly. I'm feeling much better today. You go catch your lobsters and then give me a call."

"Okay. I'll just do a short run, though, so I can be done by noon. Tell, you what—I'll bring you lunch. Takeout from the Lobster Pot. How does that sound?"

"Great! But you don't have to, Stuart. I've got plenty of food here."

"Hey, I want to see you anyway. We have a lot of stuff to talk about."

"Such as?"

"Our wedding date, for one thing."

She groaned. "I'm sorry. I know I promised to find a date, but everything's just been too crazy. Couldn't we wait for a month or two, until things calm down?"

He was silent for a minute. "Are you getting cold feet or something?"

"No, not at all. You know how I feel about you. It's just that I just have so much to do lately, I can't think straight. You know how it is in this business. It'll ease off in a couple of months."

He sounded only slightly mollified by the time he hung up, and Chelsea felt vaguely guilty for putting him off. She soothed her feelings by concentrating on calligraphy for the rest of the morning.

When she heard the knock on the door at eleven, she was completely absorbed in her work. Sitting in bed, wearing the teal-blue bathrobe, her calligraphy pens and small parchment place cards spread out before her on the small lap desk she'd had since childhood, she was inscribing name after name with flawless precision. She loved doing calligraphy, and had developed a local reputation for hand-lettered documents. Before she and Lori and Holly started Strawberry Lace, she'd made a fair amount of money penning wedding announcements and congratulatory certificates.

The sound of the knock brought her to automatic attention, and she started to her feet before the pain in her knee reminded her of her sprain. "Come in!" she called, hoping her voice was loud enough to carry through the bedroom, the living room, and the thick front door. It was probably Stuart, coming early. When she heard the door open and shut, she went back to her work. It wasn't until she caught the sound of a deeply resonant chuckle that she looked up to see Jeff Blaine standing in her bedroom doorway. He was holding a pair of crutches in one hand and a doctor's bag in the other.

"Sorry to bother you," he said, the laughter still in his voice. "Nothing even slows you down, does it?"

She was dismayed to feel the color rise in her cheeks. "I can't afford to waste any time. Your party's only three days away."

"I appreciate your dedication, but I'm sure all this can wait another twenty-four hours or so. I've made some phone calls and everybody but one on the invitation list will be attending."

"Good." She had trouble looking directly at him. His eyes had the penetrating shine that she'd always found deeply unsettling, but it was more than she could tolerate today.

He leaned the crutches against the wall and unzipped his bag. "I brought you some Ace bandages. I'll show you how to wrap them. But first I want to take a look at that knee." He drew back the blanket before she had a chance to pull down the bathrobe, which had slid up to her buttocks as she worked. He seemed amused at her consternation as she tugged it down quickly over her thighs.

"Hey, take it easy. I'm a doctor. Remember?"

All too well, she wanted to tell him. How could I forget the touch of those skilled, gentle hands?

He gently unwrapped the gauze and slid his fingers over the swelling. "Not bad. I think you're well on your way to recovery." He glanced up at her. "I'm going to show you how to wrap your own bandage and give you a couple of hints on using the crutches, and then you should be all set."

He demonstrated bandaging her knee, then unwrapped the long bandage and made her try it herself. It was more complicated than she'd realized, involving turning the strip at precisely the right points so that the bandage would support her knee while it applied pressure to reduce the swelling. He eyed her efforts critically.

"Not too bad. Try it again. A little tighter this time, but be careful not to cut off the circulation."

She did as he said, but when he insisted she do it a third time, she objected. "I really have to get back to work."

"Not until you get this right."

"What do you mean? This *is* right!" Indignant, she pushed her index finger at the bandage and then gave a cry when it hit swollen flesh.

"Hey, take it easy!" He was grinning, but there was something terribly serious in his eyes as he looked down at her. Serious and distressing. She was suddenly overwhelmed by the memory of his kiss and by a powerful desire to repeat the experience. Her hand was almost trembling as she took the bandage from him and tried to wrap it a third time. She bent over her leg, letting her hair swing forward so that she couldn't see his face, but his hands were right there in front of her, and so was the heady scent of his cologne. She could even feel the warmth of his body, pulsing in waves between them, because he was standing much too close. . . .

She stopped suddenly, dropping the bandage.

"What's wrong?"

She shook her head, pressing her hand to her mouth. He reached down, took her chin in his hand and lifted her face.

"Chelsea?"

It was something in the tone of his voice that undid her. The tears jumped into her eyes, and she didn't even know why she was crying, much less why she felt like smiling at the same time.

"This is my fault," he said quietly. "It's because of last night, isn't it?"

She nodded mutely.

"I promise you it won't happen again. You have my word on that."

Part of her wanted to tell him that the last thing she wanted was such a promise, but she kept her mouth shut and groped for a tissue.

It was while she was wiping her eyes that she heard the front door open and Stuart's hardy voice calling her name from the living room.

"Hey, Chelsea," he called again. "You should see the rusted-out Chevy Nova that's parked in front of the shop. It looks like it escaped from a junkyard."

Chapter Fourteen

JUNKYARD?" JEFF GAVE CHELSEA AN INcredulous grin.

"That's Stuart," she said quickly. "He's bringing me lunch."

"Oh." He nodded and pointed to her half-bandaged knee. "Finish wrapping that and I'll get out of your way."

Stuart appeared in the doorway, holding a brown paper bag. His face registered surprise, until Jeff turned and smiled at him warmly.

"Hi, I'm Jeff Blaine. I was just showing Chelsea how to treat her sprain."

Stuart smiled back, and they shook hands while Chelsea finally managed to wrap the bandage to Jeff's satisfaction.

"Great." Jeff zipped the black instrument bag shut and nodded to Stuart. "Nice meeting you. Congratulations on your engagement. You're a lucky man." He turned to Chelsea. "I'll check in on you later." He gave her a last, quick smile, and was gone.

Stuart frowned. "What happened to your regular doctor?"

Chelsea hesitated. "Jeff was there when I hurt myself. It turns out he's a doctor, as well as a new client."

"Client? Now I'm totally confused."

"Remember Muriel Winter's surprise party we're doing this week? Jeff is her son. I've been working with him on the planning aspects for the last two weeks."

Stuart nodded. "Well, I guess that clears up the mystery. More or less. How did he manage to turn up at the right time? He's not the same dude who rescued you at the beach, is he?"

"Actually, he is. And the same man who helped me when my van went off the road."

"Sounds like you've been needing a lot of help lately." Stuart's tone was uncharacteristically hard. "How come he always just happens to be in the area when you're in trouble?"

"I don't know! Are you suggesting this is some kind of strategy on my part?" She straightened her shoulders against the headboard and glared at him. "Because if you are, you can take your ring back this minute. I'm not interested in marrying someone who doesn't trust me!"

"What am I supposed to think? Here's this guy in your bedroom, looking at you like you're some kind of goddess or something, and your face is all flushed."

"I was crying."

His face crumpled instantly. "Jeez, I'm sorry." He set the bag on the floor and sat on the bed. He took her gently in his arms and kissed her face. "Of course I trust you, Chels."

She let out a long, shaky breath. "I don't understand what's going on. We've never fought before in our lives. What's happening?"

"I think it's called a lover's quarrel, darling." He smiled gently. "It's a sign that we're not just friends anymore."

"It's going to take some getting used to."

"For me too." He kissed her again, and she found herself kissing him back eagerly. When he finally released her, she was smiling.

"Where's the lunch you brought me? I'm starved."

Over deli tuna sandwiches they discussed the wedding.

"I really don't have many free weekends until after Labor Day," Chelsea said, studying her calendar. "Not unless I'm going to do a half-baked job on one of these parties. How about the fifteenth of September?"

"I really don't want to wait that long, Chels."

She sighed. "But what harm would it do? It would give me a chance to prepare for my own wedding, instead of cramming it in along with everything else."

"I just want to get married before the end of July."

She saw something in his eyes, a secretive flicker. "There's something you're not telling me, isn't there? There's a reason you want to get married right away." She knew instantly she was right. The flash of distress that crossed his face was unmistakable. He was hiding something. "Tell me, Stuart."

He blurted out the truth in one long breath, his sandwich clenched in his strong hand, his eyes searching the room for consolation. It was his father, he told her. He'd just been diagnosed with advanced lung cancer.

"Oh my God!" Chelsea dropped her own sandwich into her lap. She thought of the gray-haired, handsome fisherman she'd known almost all her life. "Why didn't you tell me?"

He shook his head. There were tears in his blue eyes. "He's always liked you," he said, his voice husky with emotion. "It would mean a lot to him to see our wedding."

"Of course." She reached for him and pulled him into her arms. "You should have told me earlier. Of course we'll get married right away. Before the end of the month. I promise."

They made quick, tentative plans. The wedding would be held on the lawn at Stuart's cabin; it would be a simple ceremony, with just family members as guests. There was no discussion of a honeymoon. Chelsea didn't even bring it up. Neither of them would consider leaving when Stuart's father might be near death. And they wouldn't go anywhere after he died either; his mother would need all the support she could get.

They pored over her calendar again, searching for a date. It would have to be as soon as possible after the Winter surprise party. The doctors were predicting he would last eight weeks, maybe three months at the most. They finally chose the fourth Sunday in June. It was less than three weeks away.

After Stuart left, Chelsea called Lori and told her the news. Her sister made gravely sympathetic noises about Stuart's father, but Chelsea could tell that she still had doubts about the wisdom of the marriage. It was in her voice as she congratulated her, in the careful choice of words as she asked questions about Chelsea's plans for a wedding gown.

"I won't bother with a gown. I don't have time to go through all that fussing. I'll just buy a simple white dress and a hat."

"Chels, you've always wanted a fairy-tale wedding. Remember those sketches you used to make of elaborate gowns with long trains and lace flounces?"

"I was just a kid. Besides, there's no money for that kind of dress, even if it were practical."

"Sure there's money. We're not doing the Winter surprise party for free, are we? Look, as soon as you can hobble around, we'll go to Portland and find something. Every girl deserves to have the wedding dress she's always dreamed of."

Chelsea hesitated. She was seriously tempted. Ever since Lori's wedding, when she'd helped her sister select the perfect bridal gown, she'd dreamed of shopping for her own.

"It won't hurt to look," Lori reminded her. "We'll take an afternoon off next week and go. You at least owe yourself that much. It's your *wedding,* Chels!"

"All right. But I really don't want anything too fancy."

"Of course you do! Every girl wants to look like a princess on her wedding day. And don't worry about the cake. Paul and I will take care of everything."

Chelsea called her mother, who was thrilled that Chelsea had finally set a date. She expressed sympathy for Stuart's father, then excused herself. "I have a date with Bill," she bubbled. "We're going to Kennebunkport for the afternoon."

After she hung up, Chelsea put in a call to Holly. She left a message on her answering machine, asking if she'd be her maid of honor. "The wedding's not going to be fancy, but I'd die if you weren't there. And I promise, there'll be no mention of Muriel Winter." She knew that Holly would agree to come. They'd promised each other since childhood that they'd attend each other's weddings, no matter where they were living.

Chelsea went back to her calligraphy and tried to ignore the strange sensation of alarm that gnawed at her throughout the rest of the afternoon. It was as if a small animal were running around and around inside her, trying desperately to escape.

Jeff dropped by the next morning and, after a thorough examination of her wrist and knee, pronounced her well enough to negotiate the stairs.

"Your knee healed surprisingly quickly," he said. "There's very little swelling left. How does it feel when you stand on it?"

"Better. A little tender."

He nodded. "That'll continue for a few more days. But as long as you don't do anything strenuous, I don't see why you can't resume your normal routine."

"That's a relief. I was afraid it was going to interfere with the surprise party."

"Just don't do any jogging."

Chelsea laughed. "Believe me, I won't."

"I enjoyed meeting Stuart yesterday. He seems like a good man."

"He is."

"I meant it about his being lucky."

Chelsea felt an odd wave of heat spread up her neck and into her cheeks. He was looking at her with that penetrating gaze that always unnerved her, as if he meant her to hear some unspoken words, to read the message in his dark eyes.

"You're an extraordinary woman, Chelsea. Fascinating, and very beautiful. You have a quality about you that I can't describe." He stepped closer and took her hand. " 'Garmented in light from her own beauty,' " he said softly. "I think maybe Shelley was writing about you. I hope you'll be very, very happy." Silently, he lifted her hand to his mouth and brushed his lips across her fingers. A powerful, responsive shiver ran through her. He smiled down at her knowingly. "I'd better be going. I'll see you later." He turned and quickly left her apartment. She stared after him mutely, her mind numb, her whole body trembling. She cradled her right hand in her lap. The skin on her fingers burned with a sweet, delicious heat.

By the morning of the surprise party, Chelsea was completely back on her feet. She no longer used the crutches or the Ace bandage. She was able to move around the kitchen and even climb stairs with only an occasional twinge. She had to work doubly hard, to make up for the time she'd lost, but by noon everything was ready and she and Lori were sitting in the big shop kitchen. They were waiting for Jeff's phone call, the prearranged signal indicating that he'd managed to convince his mother to go shopping with him and that the coast was clear to set up the decorations.

"We're definitely on for tomorrow afternoon," Lori reminded her. "I've already made a list of the bridal shops we're going to visit."

Chelsea grimaced. "I'm beginning to have second thoughts. It's just going to be torture for me, sis. I'll see a hundred gowns I want and not one of them will fit into the simple scheme of the wedding. I'm going to look ridiculous, all dressed up in some flowing ivory gown in front of that shabby little cabin!"

"Nonsense! You'll look beautiful! Anyway, you're going to have the ceremony down by the cove, overlooking the water, aren't you? You can hardly see the cabin from there. It'll be picture-perfect."

"I don't know. At this point, I just want to get it over with."

"Every bride feels that way. Or else she wants to get out of it altogether."

Chelsea gave her a sharp look. "I'm not trying to get out of it."

"I didn't say you were. I just meant that prenuptial jitters go with the package. How's Stuart's father doing this week?"

Chelsea sighed. "The same. He's happy about the wedding, though. He told Stuart that he's really excited about seeing the whole family together. One of his brothers is even coming from the Midwest."

The phone rang. Chelsea picked it up and heard Jeff's low voice on the other end.

"Chelsea? The coast is clear. All set?"

"All set."

"Great. I'll see you at five."

He hung up and Chelsea smiled over at Lori. "Let's roll. We have exactly four and a half hours to put it in the bag."

Everything went smoothly, from the time Chelsea pulled the van up to the service entrance of the estate and Beth Harmon greeted them at the door, to the moment the guests started arriving. At one end of the dining room, a long folding table had been set up, covered in white linen and festooned with flowers and finger foods. The oak dining table was laid with shining crystal and Muriel Winter's best china. Wheels of cheese, bowls of fresh fruit, platters of bite-sized vegetables, and an array of Strawberry Lace's most delectable hors d'oeuvres surrounded a gigantic wicker basket of fresh strawberries. A nonalcoholic bar was set up in one of the smaller dining rooms. The entire house was fragrant with the scent of fresh-cut flowers. Bouquets of roses, lilies of the valley, sweet peas, and ferns decorated fireplace mantels and side tables.

Beth took charge of the guests, directing them to remain in the dining area until she gave the signal.

At five o'clock Beth silenced everyone by ringing a small silver bell. "The car just entered the driveway," she announced. "I'm going to dim the lights now."

There were soft murmurs of excitement as the lights went out. Chelsea stood behind the buffet table with the three waitresses, while Lori waited in the kitchen. There was the sound of a car on the gravel outside, then the deep rumble of a powerful engine shutting off. Then footsteps on the gravel, approaching the dining room's French doors. She could see the figure of Muriel Winter, coming toward them. Jeff walked by her side, his hand at her elbow. Just before reaching the door, Muriel swayed and staggered. As Jeff caught and steadied her, Chelsea felt a wave of sympathetic admiration for him.

"Get ready!" Beth whispered.

The door opened, the lights went on, and there was a sudden shout of "Surprise!" and then everyone was laughing and Muriel Winter was standing in the doorway with a stunned expression on her face.

It took only moments for her to collect herself, and then she was the same, elegant woman that Chelsea remembered from the Columbus Day party two and a half years ago. She bowed and swept and danced her way through the room, greeting people, laughing, nodding, chatting casually, while Jeff stood grinning triumphantly over at Chelsea. He cornered her in the small dining room a short time later, when she was stocking the bar with clean glasses.

"I think it's working," he said. "I haven't seen her this happy since I came back from Africa."

"Wonderful." Chelsea picked up a dirty glass from the windowsill. She gave him a quick smile, then glanced away, unnerved by his closeness and the intimacy of his look.

"She's already had people ask when she's holding her next party. That's a good sign."

Chelsea nodded and tried to slide past him to the door.

He put his hand on her arm. "Is something wrong?"

"No. What could be wrong?"

"I don't know. You seem uneasy, apprehensive or something. What is it?"

She looked up at him. His eyes were shining and he was smiling at her with that gorgeous dimple showing. How on earth could she tell him that *he* was the reason she was uneasy? "It's nothing, honestly. I just have a lot of work to do."

He let her go, but she was intensely aware of his gaze all evening. It seemed as if, whenever they were in the same room together, his eyes never left her. She was relieved when the guests finally started leaving and she could retreat to the sanctuary of the kitchen.

She felt better as she began the arduous clean-up task. She told herself firmly she was imagining things, that Jeff had merely been happy that the party had gone so well. And she almost had herself convinced. Until Beth popped into the kitchen and informed her in a worried tone that Mrs. Winter wanted to speak to her privately.

Beth led her to the solarium, where Muriel was seated in a large, wicker chair. Like a queen on a throne, thought Chelsea. And I'm just a lowly serf come to pay my respects.

"Mrs. Winter?" She wiped her hands nervously on her apron. "You wanted to see me?"

Muriel fixed her with a blue-eyed stare. "Yes. Sit down."

Chelsea sat in a chair next to a giant fern. The solarium was dimly lit by small lamps set on low tables. Through the glass she could see stars in the black sky and the glint of water in the distance. "What can I do for you?"

"I have two things, Miss Adams. First, I wish to compliment you on the fine work Strawberry Lace has done tonight. My son has indicated his desire that we renegotiate our contract for the Fourth of July, and I've promised him I'll consider it."

"Thank you."

Muriel held up her hand. "Which brings me to my second point." She leaned forward, her sharp elbows propped on the brown wicker arms. "I believe I have been plain with you in the past about your relationship with Jefferson. My concerns have not changed. I have seen nothing this evening to make me question those concerns."

Chelsea straightened her shoulders. "I'm afraid I don't understand."

"I believe you do. All evening, you have been enticing him to play the fool."

"Fool?"

"Exactly. You've entranced him, swept him off his feet. And I will not see my son seduced by a woman of no social standing. I will not—"

"Mother!" Jeff's sharp voice cut her off. Chelsea's jaw dropped as she turned to watch him stride into the room, his shoulders squared, his face dark with anger. "What do you think you're doing?"

Muriel recovered her composure instantly. "I'm speaking to one of the workers, Jefferson. Please leave us alone."

"No. I will not leave you alone. You're embarrassing yourself. And me as well." He looked at Chelsea. "I apologize. My mother is not herself right now. The party has tired her more than I realized."

"It hasn't tired me!" Muriel's voice was a hiss. "It's rejuvenated me. Now, please allow me to finish."

"No," said Jeff. "Chelsea, you're free to leave."

"Excuse me, but I'd like to say something." Chelsea stood up slowly. "Mrs. Winter, we've spoken about your concerns in the past and I believe I made it clear then that I have no romantic interest in your son." She felt Jeff's eyes on her as she continued. "I'm engaged to be married and the wedding date has been set. By the time of your Independence Day party—assuming you decide to host a party—I will be Mrs. Stuart Potter. I hope that relieves your mind."

As she turned and quickly left the room, Chelsea caught a glimpse of Jeff's shocked face; his dark eyes were following her sadly.

Chapter Fifteen

CHELSEA WAS TREMBLING WITH OUTRAGE as she hurried down the long hall to the kitchen. She had never felt more deeply humiliated in her life. It had been all she could do to control herself as she spoke to Muriel Winter; she'd had to push her hands down hard into her apron pockets to keep from smashing them into the woman's haughty face.

Tears suddenly filled her eyes and she ducked into a small sitting room to collect herself. The last thing she wanted was to let Lori see her like this. She found a tissue in her pocket, wiped her eyes, blew her nose, then wiped her eyes again. She smoothed her hair, took a deep breath, and was just turning back to the door when Jeff appeared. Pale and out of breath, he braced his hands against the door frame, blocking her way.

Her first thought was that he wanted an apology. She'd been too disrespectful of his mother's authority; walking out without being dismissed verged on impertinence. But when she started to explain why she'd left the solarium so hurriedly, he cut her off.

"You're getting married this *month?*"

"Yes."

"But I thought you just became engaged a few days ago."

"I did." She tried to keep the tremor out of her voice. "But I've known Stuart for years."

"But you can't. . . ." He paused. "Don't you have to make a lot of arrangements first? Aren't there things that need to be done?"

"Not that much, really."

"You make it sound like this is an emergency."

"It is, sort of."

His glance slid to her abdomen and she colored instantly.

"I'm not pregnant, if that's what you're thinking."

"Then why the rush?"

"That's really my business, isn't it?"

He stared at her. He was still blocking the doorway.

"Excuse me." She tried to step past him, but he came into the room and closed the door before she could leave.

She frowned. "I have to get back to the kitchen."

"Not until we talk. Sit down."

She crossed her arms over her breasts. "I have at least two hours of work ahead of me before I can even think of going home tonight. I'd like to get at it."

He pointed to the couch. "Sit down." There was something in his tone that told her she'd better do as he said. She sat, and he began pacing back and forth in front of her, his hands pushed deep into the pockets of his slacks. He was frowning in concentration, his head bent as he spoke. "I don't quite know how to say this without sounding arrogant, but you're making a mistake."

"A mistake?"

"Rushing into marriage is never a good idea."

"Are you an expert or something?"

"No." His voice was low. "I'm not an expert at all. I'm just someone who happens to care."

She felt like she'd been slapped, and it was doubly painful because she knew she deserved it. "I'm sorry. I didn't mean that the way it sounded. It's just that I've had so much advice from people lately, I'm beginning to wonder if I have an opinion of my own."

He took a step toward her. She thought at first that he was going to say something, but as she gazed up into his dark eyes, she realized that what he wanted to tell her was beyond words. She felt her whole body vibrate in response to his scrutiny, as if she were a harp and his eyes a pair of stroking hands. He reached out, and she was surprised to find her own hand meeting his. She stared up at him in astonishment as he pulled her gently to her feet.

"My mother's right, you know," he said softly. "I do look at you in a certain way. It makes her nervous for a very good reason." He drew her closer, lifted her hand to his lips, turned it over and kissed the palm. A shock wave swept through her; she shook with the intensity of her response. He released her hand and cupped her chin, tilting her head to his. "You *have* swept me off my feet. I'm completely under your spell."

As he bent to kiss her, Chelsea felt as if she were in a wonderful dream; everything was moving slowly and smoothly toward a sweet, unavoidable conclusion. Her lips met his eagerly, and she lifted her hands to pull his head closer and stroke the strong column of his neck. His hands moved down her back, over the swell of her hips. His tongue found hers and caressed it tenderly; she gave a little moan and pressed herself urgently against him.

She knew he was pulling her down onto the couch, knew that his fingers were undoing the buttons of her blouse, and yet she had no wish to stop him. Her mind was empty of everything but her own overpowering desire. It wasn't until he was sliding his hand over the curve of her breast and around her back to unhook her bra that she came to.

"Wait," she said in a choked voice. "I can't do this. Please stop."

He released her slowly and sat up. "I know I promised this wouldn't happen again. It's just . . ." He paused, shook his head. "I don't know what it is about you, Chelsea, but I can't seem to control myself when I'm near you. Something comes over me. It's overwhelming. I'm sorry."

She couldn't look straight at him because of the open pain in his eyes. She concentrated on buttoning her blouse.

"You're not like any other woman I've ever met. I've never had this reaction before. When I'm with you, I feel excited, happy, thrilled to just be alive. You're light to my fire, words to my music." He gave a low chuckle. "It's funny; the words to all those corny old love songs suddenly make sense to me."

The violent trembling she'd experienced earlier returned. She sat up and smoothed her skirt over her knees. She didn't know if she could talk, if her voice would even work if she tried. She forced herself to look at him and was instantly sorry, because he was smiling at her with a gaze so tender that her breath locked in her throat.

"I'm afraid I've fallen in love with you, Chelsea Adams," he whispered.

"Don't." She shook her head. "Please don't . . ."

He took her hand tenderly between his, bent over the cup of his palms and kissed her fingers. "I'm sorry. I can't help it."

She took a deep, shuddering breath. "You have to. I'm in love with another man."

"Are you? Truly?"

"Yes."

"Then why do you respond to me the way you do? Why do you kiss me so sweetly?"

She swallowed. "I don't know," she said hoarsely. "It's just some kind of fluke, I guess. A crazy chemistry—"

"It more than chemistry, Chelsea." His gaze was piercing.

She pulled her hand out of his and stood up, praying that he wouldn't notice her shaking knees. "Anyway, it doesn't matter. I'm getting married very soon."

He sighed and got slowly to his feet. "You're right. And the worst of it is, I can't even bring myself to dislike your fiancé. He seems like a perfectly nice guy."

"He is. He's wonderful. And he makes me very happy."

He gazed at her for a long moment before he spoke. "Then your wedding date is definite."

"Yes, it is."

He nodded slowly. "I'm sorry I tried to interfere, Chelsea. Honestly. Please accept my apology."

"Of course." She nodded stiffly and went to the door. Her movements felt jerky, uneven. She was aware of the heat of his gaze on her back, as if his eyes were burning two round holes right between the tight muscles of her shoulder blades.

* * *

Lori was working at the kitchen sink when Chelsea came in. "I was beginning to wonder if Muriel had tied you to a torture rack in her basement or something. I was just about to come looking for you. What major sin did you commit?"

"Imagined sin is more like it." Chelsea opened a cupboard and started putting away clean glasses from the dishwasher. She prayed that Lori couldn't detect the agitation in her voice. "The woman's having delusions. You won't believe it if I tell you."

"Tell me anyway."

"She's afraid I'm going to seduce her precious son." She waited for Lori's laugh, but it didn't come. Chelsea glanced at her sister. She was wiping her hands on her apron, looking straight at her. Her expression was solemn.

"I have to be honest with you, Chels. I couldn't help noticing the way you and Jeff look at each other. Maybe Muriel's right to be nervous."

"Give me a break, Lori. You know how I feel about what happened to Holly. I'm smart enough to stay away from any situation that involves a son of Muriel Winter."

"We're not talking about intelligence here. The best intentions in the world can't control your true feelings."

"What true feelings?"

"I think you're falling in love with Jeff Blaine."

"That's ridiculous! That's absolutely the *last* thing I'd ever do in my life!"

"Love isn't something you can control. It just *happens* to you. It takes you over." Lori crossed the room and put a gentle hand on Chelsea's shoulder. "You shouldn't fight it, Chels. You'll just make yourself miserable, not to mention everyone else around you."

Tears welled suddenly into Chelsea's eyes as she turned to face her sister. "I have to fight it," she whispered. "I can't do this to Stuart—"

"You can't keep it from him, Chels. You owe him the truth." Lori put her arms around her gently.

Chelsea's tears overflowed and spilled down her cheeks. "You don't understand. Even if I weren't marrying Stuart, Jeff and I couldn't . . ." She wiped desperately at her tears. ". . . we couldn't see each other. Muriel's promised to destroy Strawberry Lace if I ever have anything to do with him."

Lori's eyes widened. "What?"

"If I ever have a romantic relationship with Jeff, she'll see to it that our business—the business we've both put so much work and money and love into—is destroyed."

"She actually said that?" Lori handed her a tissue. "Oh, Chelsea, you poor thing! Why didn't you tell me?"

"I didn't want to upset you. With the baby coming and all, you need to stay calm."

"But I thought we had a rule that we'd share everything in this business. Haven't we always faced the hard times together?"

Chelsea nodded as she wiped her eyes.

"Then we can do it now too. One woman, even if she's as rich and powerful as Muriel Winter, can't destroy everything we've worked so hard to build for the last four years. She might keep us from getting as far as we'd like, but she won't destroy us."

"I wish I could believe you."

"You can. Look, if worse comes to worst, we'll take on a new name, hire a P.R. consultant. We'll do what we have to do. But we're not going to let Muriel Winter run our lives."

Chelsea gave her sister a forlorn smile. "Well, I'm going to make sure she doesn't have any cause to. Once I'm wearing a wedding ring, she'll see for herself that I'm no threat to her son."

Lori stared. "You mean you're still going through with the wedding? Even though you just admitted your feelings for Jeff?"

Chelsea nodded as she wiped away the last of her tears. "Nothing's changed. I'm not going to throw away the business and my relationship with Stuart just because of my feelings."

Lori scowled. "You've always been stubborn, but this is downright stupid. You're in love with this handsome, sexy—not to mention *wealthy*—man who can't keep his eyes off you, and you're going to marry a friend you met in high school?" Her voice rose in a little squeak.

"I never said I was in love with him. And anyway, the wedding may be the last day Dan Potter gets to see his whole family. I'm not going to take that away from him."

Lori shook her head sadly. "I don't believe you're saying these things. This is insane."

"Look, Lori, I decided a long time ago that I'm not going to follow in Mom's footsteps and go mooning around in a daze all the time over some guy who happens to smile at me. I had a good taste of romance in college when I thought I was in love with Noah. It's not what it's cracked up to be; I found that out the hard way I don't need a remedial lesson."

"You were eighteen. And Noah Richards was an egotistical creep. That doesn't prove anything about love."

"It proves that I can't trust my feelings."

"All right, go ahead and ruin your life. See if I care."

"I'm hardly ruining my life. I'm marrying my best friend in the world. Stuart and I are soul mates. Anyway, even if Stuart weren't in the picture, I wouldn't marry Jeff—not even if his mother gave us her blessing."

"Why on earth not?"

"Because I'd *die* before I'd put myself in a situation where I had Muriel Winter for a mother-in-law!"

There was a scraping sound behind them, and Chelsea whirled to find Muriel standing in the doorway. She was staring straight at Chelsea, her small blue eyes hard as ice chips, her haughty face a mask of disdain.

Lori was the first to collect herself. "Is there something we can do for you, Mrs. Winter?"

A small smile appeared on the thin lips. "I came to congratulate you on your work this evening." Her gaze didn't waver from Chelsea. "And I applaud your convictions, Miss Adams. They are comparable to my own. Our feelings are, I assure you, most definitely mutual. I must say, you have greatly relieved my mind." She turned and withdrew from the room, leaving the door swinging quietly behind her.

Lori stared at Chelsea in horror. "What are we going to do?"

"I don't know. Go after her?"

"Maybe we should just leave and send her a note of apology tomorrow. Give her a chance to cool down."

"It probably won't do any good."

Lori nodded. "Maybe not, but we don't have much choice, do we?"

"Oh, Lori, I'm so sorry!" Chelsea threw her arms around her sister. Her tears returned, spilling down her cheeks. "I've made such a mess of everything!"

Lori made soothing sounds and patted her back in true, big-sisterly fashion, but Chelsea knew from the tone of her voice that her sister was just as scared and mortified as she was.

Chelsea slept restlessly and woke late the next morning wondering how to phrase an apology to Muriel Winter. She knew it was probably a useless effort, that Muriel was undoubtedly already spreading the word among her elite friends that Strawberry Lace was a catering service to avoid at all costs. There was probably no point in starting work on the Independence Day party plans either, as she'd planned to do that day. She might as well use the day to plan her own wedding. She hadn't been completely honest when she'd told Jeff there wasn't much to do. Even with a small, family wedding, there were hundreds of little details that had to be addressed.

She called Lori, asked if she was free to go into Portland. "You promised me a shopping trip," she said. "I'm in the market for a wedding gown."

"Really? I thought you were going to make do with a white dress."

"I probably am, but I really need a break today, and bridal-gown shopping sounds like fun. Are you up to it?"

"You bet, Chels." She could hear the smile in Lori's voice. "I wouldn't miss it for the world."

They took Chelsea's car to Portland, because Lori

was starting to have trouble fitting behind the wheel of her Ford Taurus.

"And I'm only starting my eighth month!" she complained. "I'm going to look like a giant pumpkin before this thing is over!"

Chelsea laughed. "Are you sure it's not twins?"

"The doctor keeps telling me there's only one baby in there. He must be a monster!"

"Watch out world, here comes Junior LeBlanc!"

The shopping trip proved to be a wonderful tonic to Chelsea's spirits. They started at the Maine Mall and then drove into Portland to cover the bridal shops there. Just before noon she spotted her dream dress in a little boutique in the Old Port district.

The gown was displayed on a wire-framed mannequin in the far back corner of the shop. It was a froth of satin and ivory lace, yards and yards of delicate fabric cascading from the pearl-beaded bodice. Long lace gloves and an illusion veil on a circlet of white silk roses completed the outfit. Chelsea stood in front of it, her eyes shining.

"I wonder how much it costs," she mused.

"Don't even ask," Lori advised. "You're going to take it. It's perfect."

"I can't take it if I can't pay for it." She turned to the clerk, who was smiling at her eagerly.

"You have excellent taste, miss. This is an original Paulette creation, hand-beaded, lined with silk—"

"How much?"

"Only one thousand, five hundred dollars."

Chelsea's eyes widened in shock. "Fifteen hundred dollars! For one dress?"

"It's a bridal gown, miss. Made for the most important day in your life."

Chelsea gazed at the gown and imagined herself

wearing it, walking down the lawn behind Stuart's cabin. She pictured the sea breeze lifting the veil and teasing her hair, imagined how the satin would make soft, whispering sounds as she moved. She wanted it desperately, but she couldn't afford fifteen hundred dollars for a dress she would wear only once in her life. She shook her head. "I can't—"

"Try it on," Lori urged. "Don't say no before you try it on."

Half an hour later Chelsea was standing in front of a triptych of mirrors, her skin glowing, her smile radiant. "It's perfect!" she whispered. "It's the gown I've always dreamed of!" She felt ravishing and fragile and utterly feminine inside the cascading lace. She closed her eyes and imagined holding a bouquet of fresh wildflowers, walking across a lush green lawn toward her groom. Through the veil, she could see the soft blur of faces, hear the cry of sea gulls overhead, hear the wedding march being played exquisitely on an electronic keyboard. She approached the minister, where the groom waited to lift her veil. The music stopped, her veil rose, and she looked up into Jeff's handsome face—

Her eyes snapped open. "I can't take it," she said quickly. "It's not right."

"But you just said it was perfect!" Lori protested. "You have to buy it!"

"No." Chelsea shook her head firmly. "I've changed my mind. It's not the right dress for my wedding." And she hurried into the dressing room to take it off before anyone could see the tears shining in her eyes.

Chapter Sixteen

"I CAN'T BELIEVE YOU LEFT THAT GORgeous dress in the shop and bought that plain little knee-length thing at Sears!" Lori wailed as Chelsea swung the car onto the southbound ramp of the interstate. "So what if the wedding's going to be small? It's *your* wedding."

Chelsea tightened her hands on the wheel. "I don't want to talk about it anymore."

"Suit yourself. But I put the dream dress on layaway for you, just in case you change your mind."

"You *what?*"

"While you were changing into your clothes, I put a small deposit on it. My treat. Look, Paul and I will be happy to help pay for it—"

"No! Absolutely not! End of discussion." Chelsea eased into the acceleration lane, watching for traffic.

"Don't get in a snit about it. I'm not going to force it down your throat or anything."

"I'm sorry, sis. I guess I'm just tense. Look, I have an idea. Why don't we take a day off and go out to Eagle Island? We could both use a change of scene."

"What about Muriel Winter's Independence Day party?"

"Are you kidding? After what happened last night, I'm sure that's cancelled."

Lori sighed. "I guess you're right."

"I'll get Stuart to take us out to the island tomorrow morning. We'll pack a lunch and make a day of it. How does that sound?"

Lori shrugged.

"You like it out there as much as I do. Come on, we deserve a vacation day. Look at it this way: it may be the last time you get to go out there without lugging a baby."

Lori laughed. "I already am lugging a baby. But you've got a point. Okay, you're on."

There were two calls on her answering machine when Chelsea let herself into the apartment. The first was from Holly, saying she was thrilled that Chelsea was getting married, and that she'd be delighted to be her maid of honor. The second was Beth Harmon, calling for Muriel Winter.

"Mrs. Winter wishes to make it clear she will not be needing your services in the future." The machine clicked off.

Although she'd expected it, Chelsea's heart sank. Their one big chance to grow into an elite catering business was gone. And it was all her fault. She hadn't been able to contain her contempt for Muriel Winter, and she was reaping the bitter harvest.

She called Lori and told her the bad news. After a short silence her sister rallied. "All the more reason we should go out to the island tomorrow, like you suggested. It'll clear our minds, give us something to do besides sit around and mope. Have you called Stuart?"

"Not yet, but I'm sure he'll say yes."

But Stuart surprised her by his reluctance. "Tomorrow's Sunday," he reminded her. "You know I don't haul on Sundays."

"So spend the day on the island with us. Come on, Stuart. Lori and I really need to get out on the water." She explained what had happened to Strawberry Lace.

Stuart sighed. "I wish I could help you out, Chels, but I promised my father I'd spend the afternoon with him." His voice thickened suddenly. "He's back in the hospital. He had a bad reaction to the chemotherapy."

"Oh, Stuart! I'm sorry. If I'd known, I wouldn't have suggested—"

"No, it's okay. I could probably take you out there in the morning and then pick you up before dark. Maybe it would take my mind off Dad for a couple of hours."

"Are you sure? I don't want to add to your burdens."

"You could never do that, Chels."

"I feel so bad about your father," Chelsea said. "I was hoping for some good news for a change."

"The good news is our wedding, Chels. It's the one thing he's really looking forward to. And so am I."

"Me too," she said.

The wind was gusting hard under a gray sky when *Chelsea's Choice* headed out of Bryant's Cove early the next morning. Chelsea was glad that she and Lori had thought to wear sweaters over their blouses. Even in mid-June, mornings on the coast of Maine could be downright chilly. Stuart kept looking doubtfully at the sky. As they rounded a ledge and moved into the open water of Casco Bay, he pointed to a band of dark clouds lying on the horizon, far out to sea.

"Looks like it's thinking about blowing up a real storm. I'm not sure I like the idea of leaving you two alone on the island."

"We'll be fine," Chelsea insisted. "Besides, what can happen on the island? We'll be safer there than on the *Chelsea*."

Stuart grunted skeptically.

"Look, if it rains, we'll just wait at the house. It's got a nice, deep porch; we won't get wet."

He scowled, but she wrapped her arms around him from behind and stood on tiptoe to kiss the back of his neck, and a few minutes later he was laughing.

The island was deserted when they arrived. Stuart helped them stow their food and a couple of extra blankets in the dingy. As they kissed good-bye, she reflected on how safe and secure she felt in his arms. It was a good feeling, better in a lot of ways than the unsettling passion she experienced in Jeff's embrace. It was certainly far more soothing. They were both smiling as he helped Lori into the dingy, then handed Chelsea the oars. She rowed quickly in to the little beach, where she and Lori climbed out, hauled the boat high up on the sand, and secured it to a rock. She waved to Stuart as he swung *Chelsea's Choice* around, and then she and Lori carried their things up to the house.

They were surprised and pleased to find that the building was open. "The park ranger must have forgotten to lock it up yesterday," Lori said as they entered the dark-paneled living room.

The large building had been built as a summer home for Robert Peary, the Arctic explorer credited with discovering the North Pole. It was here, on this small, green island, that he planned his expeditions. The house had been preserved in its original decor, and always struck Chelsea as a forbidding place, with its dark walls and menacing stuffed animal heads. There was a summer-camp feel about it: informal and breezy, with long, glassed-in porches and creaking wooden floors. Upstairs, a chain of small bedrooms was tucked under the eaves.

They placed their food and blankets in a corner of the living room and explored the house lingeringly, though they'd visited it many times before. When they came back outside, Chelsea noticed that the band of dark clouds on the horizon had widened. The wind was blowing up whitecaps on the water, and every few minutes an unusually high swell would hit the rocks east of the house with a crash, sending spray frothing into the air.

"Looks like we'd better take a walk around the island while we still can," Chelsea said. "Maybe this wasn't such a good idea."

"Of course it was a good idea. Look at it this way: the clouds will keep the tourists away. We'll have the island all to ourselves."

It gratified Chelsea to see Lori in such high spirits. It made her feel more optimistic herself. Maybe it was all part of Lori's big-sister consolation plan, but it was working. Within minutes they were laughing happily as they hiked the wooded path that circled the little island.

They stopped to gather a few wild strawberries, which Chelsea spotted near a narrow rock outcropping. "I know we're not supposed to do this, but if we don't taste a couple, I'll never forgive myself. I *adore* wild strawberries." She grinned at Lori. "Think we could come up with a recipe for wild strawberry blini?"

"Why not?"

"Maybe you can make some for my wedding."

"Give me a break, Chels! Where am I going to find enough wild strawberries to serve a crowd?"

"Maybe just two, then—one for the bride and groom and one for everybody else."

They continued along the path, laughing and chatting. It felt good to be away from all their responsibilities, to savor the sights and sounds and smells of the sea and the exquisite beauty of the small green island. When they had circled the island twice, Lori suggested they return to the house; she wanted to get off her feet for a while. As they came out of the woods and climbed the lawn behind the house, Chelsea spotted the white mast of a sailboat moored in the little cove.

"Damn! Somebody else is here." She pointed the boat out to Lori.

"The place is big enough for both of us, I think," Lori said brightly. "It's not as if it's crawling with people the way it sometimes is."

Chelsea shrugged and accompanied her sister up to the porch, where they sat on a narrow wooden bench and gazed out to sea. The sky had darkened considerably since their arrival, and patches of fog obscured the nearby islands. But to Chelsea the view was stunning. She'd never understood some people's conviction that the ocean was only beautiful on bright summer days. That was when all the pictures were taken, of course; it was the ocean that people painted. But she'd always relished the stark beauty of an approaching storm. The water had a gray-green cast, with swirling blue shadows just under the surface. Gulls swooped and cried, their gray and white bodies mirroring the choppy sea. The surf boomed against the cliff. She took a deep breath, let it out slowly.

"This is wonderful," she said. "I already feel better."

"I wish I could say the same." Lori was hunched forward, her face drawn into a pinched expression.

"What's wrong?"

"I don't know. I'm not feeling very well all of a sudden."

"Do you want to lie down?"

Lori shook her head. "Actually, I felt better when we were walking. Maybe we should walk some more."

"Whatever feels right." Chelsea followed her sister across the porch to the steps. "Let's go down on the beach."

Lori appeared to be having a hard time negotiating the stairs. She stopped halfway down and clutched her swollen belly.

"What is it?" Chelsea was instantly beside her. "Are you in pain?"

"Sort of." Lori's eyes were round with anxiety. "If I didn't know better, I'd think I just had a contraction."

"A *contraction?*" Chelsea's own stomach clenched in alarm. "You mean you think you're in labor?"

"I can't be. I'm only eight months along." Lori grunted and descended the rest of the steps quickly. "I feel better now. It was probably just indigestion."

They walked down onto the beach. Chelsea tossed some stones into the water, while Lori gathered periwinkle shells. The clouds had thickened and darkened ominously, and the wind was stronger. The sailboat rocked wildly on its mooring. Out of the corner of her eye Chelsea caught a flash of lightning to the east. She turned to see a curtain of rain running toward them over the water.

"We'd better head back to the house or we're going to get soaked." She looked back at Lori, who was standing, frozen, her hands clutched together over her stomach, her eyes fixed on a point in the air a few feet in front of her.

"Lori?" She ran over to her, but Lori didn't acknowledge her, didn't shift her eyes or move a muscle. She just stood there, paralyzed, staring at nothing.

"Lori! Talk to me!" Chelsea put her hand on her sister's shoulder, which seemed to break the spell. Lori looked at her. Her face was pale and there was fear in her eyes.

"I think maybe it *is* labor," she said in a choked voice.

A low roll of thunder sounded, and Chelsea felt the first raindrop hit her arm. She put her arm around her sister. "Come on, we have to get you inside."

The sky was so dark now, it was like walking at dusk. Chelsea kept her eyes on the path and guided Lori along, stopping whenever her sister's sharp intake of breath signaled the arrival of another contraction.

The rain started in earnest, showering them with hard, fat drops; the wind whipped their hair and clothes angrily. They reached the porch just as it began to pour; relentless sheets of cold water sliced savagely through the dark air.

* * *

Chelsea helped Lori up the narrow stairs to a tiny bedroom and persuaded her to lie down. Lori was curled on her side, breathing through a long contraction, when Chelsea heard someone enter the building. She had a wild hope that it was Stuart, and started eagerly down the stairs to greet him. But as she turned the corner of the landing, she heard the sound of a woman's voice. She froze, her hand clutching the stair railing. Of course, she told herself; it couldn't be Stuart. He was probably already in Portland, and it was unlikely that the storm had reached the mainland. Even if he were still on the water, he was an expert navigator who didn't take chances. The prospect of a thunderstorm would have sent him to the closest harbor to ride out the storm. She bent and peered into the shadowy room below.

Two figures—a man and a woman—were bending over something near the door.

"Hello?" she said.

The figures straightened and turned and then one of them flicked on a flashlight. Chelsea gasped. The man was Jeff Blaine and the woman was his mother.

"Chelsea?" Jeff's voice was puzzled. "What are you doing here?"

"Jeff!" She ran down the rest of the stairs. "Thank God, it's you! How did you get here?"

"We made the mistake of taking a morning sail." He came toward her quickly. Behind him, Muriel stood with her hand braced against the door, glaring. "I was surprised to find the building open. I didn't expect anyone would be here. Don't tell me you rowed all the way out here in that little skiff."

She shook her head. "Stuart dropped us off."

"Us?"

"My sister's upstairs. She's . . . I think she's in labor." Chelsea grabbed his arm. "You're a doctor. You can help her. Please. She's in a lot of pain." She started tugging him toward the stairs, but Muriel's sharp voice stopped them.

"Jefferson, would you kindly give me your arm?"

Jeff turned briefly. "Chelsea can help you find a place to sit. There's a woman in labor upstairs." He placed his hand over Chelsea's and bent to speak in her ear. "She's having trouble walking today. Just support her left side and guide her to one of the chairs." He gave her hand a little squeeze, then ran past her up the stairs.

Chelsea reluctantly offered her arm to Muriel. The woman's hand was cold and clawlike; she clutched Chelsea's arm with an intensity that brought tears to her eyes. Chelsea had an impulse to yank her arm away, but remembered the concern in Jeff's request and forced herself to lead the woman to a wide-backed wicker chair near the row of windows. She had to swallow her antipathy as Muriel swayed against her with each step. When she was finally seated, Chelsea asked if there was anything else she could do.

"Yes," Muriel snapped. "Get me a blanket. I saw some over there in the corner."

"Those are ours." The words popped out before Chelsea could consider how childish they sounded. She clamped her mouth shut and went to retrieve a blanket, which she draped carefully over Muriel's legs. "There. Is there anything else?" Impatient to get back upstairs to Lori, she almost screamed when Muriel ordered her to locate a battery-operated lamp. "There's one over there, among the things we brought in from the boat." She pointed toward the door.

Chelsea had trouble finding the lamp, because the light outside had grown so murky with clouds and rain. But she finally located it at the bottom of a knapsack. It was a small table lamp mounted on a battery. She flicked it on and brought it to Muriel.

"If you're all set for a few minutes, I'll go back and check on my sister."

"Wait." The clawlike hand grabbed Chelsea's wrist. "Don't leave me."

Chelsea started to draw her arm back and open her mouth to deliver a sharp retort, when she noticed something startling in Muriel's face.

It seemed so out of place that for a moment she didn't recognize it. And when she did, she had to look again to be sure of what she was seeing. But it was definitely there, etched plainly on the aristocratic face: the stark, potent emotion of fear.

Chapter Seventeen

WHEN JEFF CAME DOWNSTAIRS, CHELSEA was sitting in the light of the little lamp, holding Muriel's hand and reassuring her about the sturdiness of the Peary house. "It's withstood hundreds of northeasters, even hurricanes," she said. "This is just a little storm. We won't even feel it."

Jeff had taken off his sweater and rolled his shirtsleeves to the elbows. "Your sister's in labor, all right," he told Chelsea. "She's already four centimeters dilated. That baby's on its way." He raked a hand through his hair. "I'm going to need your help. Yours too, Mother."

"Mine?" Muriel frowned. "What can I do?"

"You can help Chelsea make up a bed, for starters. I'm going to bring a mattress down here so Lori can deliver the baby in this room."

"Here?" Muriel's eyes widened.

"It's the best place. We can build a fire in the fireplace to take the chill off. If we all stay in this room, just our combined body heat should help keep the baby warm." He turned to Chelsea. "Look around and see what you can find in the way of blankets, towels, sheets, anything we can use for warmth."

Chelsea nodded. "Is she going to be all right?"

"It's a normal labor, as far as I can tell at this point."

"Shouldn't we be boiling some water?" Muriel asked.

"Why? I don't have any instruments to sterilize."

"What about cleaning up afterward?"

"Good point. Maybe we can heat some water over the fire. I'll go get that mattress and we can bring Lori down here where she belongs." Jeff hurried back up the stairs.

"My son is a very good doctor, you know," Muriel said. "He's delivered hundreds of babies. Your sister will be all right."

"Thanks." Chelsea gave her a weak smile. "I'll go see what I can find."

"If you'll bring my things over here, I might be able to locate something that will be of use."

Chelsea carried the two knapsacks to Muriel and went to explore the house. She stripped the upstairs beds of blankets, and found two afghans in an ancient trunk. A kitchen drawer contained three dish towels, and she found a quilt in a cupboard above a narrow counter. When she returned to the central room, Muriel had located three flashlights, two large beach towels, and a box of kitchen matches. Jeff had brought a mattress downstairs and laid it in front of the fireplace. Muriel was on her knees beside it, spreading a big towel over the musty blanket.

She looked up as Chelsea came in. "These towels are the cleanest things we have. We'll use one under your sister and the other to wrap the baby." She started to push herself to her feet, but her right leg buckled and she sagged back onto her knees.

Chelsea reached to help her. Muriel hesitated a moment, then accepted her hand.

"Thank you." She swayed heavily against Chelsea as she rose, and Chelsea had to catch her with her free arm to keep the older woman from falling. She guided her back to the wicker chair and was settling her into it when Jeff appeared on the landing.

"If everything's all set, I'm going to bring her down. Chelsea, could you give me a hand?"

She ran up the stairs, to find Lori sitting on the bed, looking pale and frightened. Her maternity slacks had been removed and she was wearing only the long, loose sweater she'd put on that morning.

"It's okay, sis," Chelsea said reassuringly. "Everything's going to be fine. Jeff's a great doctor."

Lori nodded. "I'm just worried about the baby. He's not due for another month."

"I think your obstetrician may have miscalculated the date," Jeff told her. "That feels like a full-term baby to me."

"I hope you're right."

"Well, if I'm not, maybe it will reassure you to know that I've delivered a lot of premature babies under primitive conditions. I've learned how to improvise." He patted Lori's shoulder. "We're going to link arms and make a chair for you now. I don't want to risk a fall." He nodded to Chelsea. "Okay, let's go."

They worked their way carefully down the stairs and settled Lori on the mattress, propping her back on a thick roll of blankets. She had another contraction immediately, and Chelsea watched with alarm as

Lori's hands locked into white fists and she moaned through clenched teeth.

"Take it easy," Jeff said, squatting beside her. "Breathe through the contraction, like I told you. Breathe. Breathe. That's it. That's very good." He signaled to Chelsea. "Here. Make sure she takes slow, deep breaths when she feels a contraction coming. I'm going to build a fire."

Chelsea followed his instructions, sitting on the floor beside her sister, holding her hand, trying to help focus Lori's attention away from the intense pain building in her uterus. When the contraction finally eased, Lori blew out a long breath and sagged back onto the mattress.

"Whew!" she whispered. "That was a hard one."

"You're doing great, sis. Everything's going just fine."

"How would you know?" Lori gave her a wry grin.

"Sisterly intuition."

She heard Jeff's chuckle behind her and turned. He was squatting in front of the fireplace, stacking pieces of wood in a small fortlike pattern. "That's as good an answer as any I've heard," he said. He lit a match, held it to the tiny scraps of kindling at the base of his creation. "Here's hoping."

A few minutes later a crackling fire was brightening the dark room, throwing a warm orange glow over the occupants.

Jeff put his hand on Chelsea's shoulder. "I need to talk with you a minute," he said. "Alone."

She followed him quickly out of the room and through another room to a long, glassed-in corridor overlooking the ocean. She looked up at him anxiously. "Something's wrong, isn't it?"

He shook his head. "I just wanted to let you know what we're in for. Have you ever witnessed a birth?"

"No."

"It's going to get a little rough in the next couple of hours. She'll go through a period of irritability; it'll be hard for her to concentrate on her breathing, even with our help, and she won't feel like she can do what's required of her. She may scream or cry, but I don't want you to worry. It's all perfectly normal."

Chelsea nodded slowly.

"Thanks for sitting with my mother. I know . . ." He paused and glanced out at the water. "I know how you must feel about her after what happened yesterday. But she's not entirely herself these days. She's been having a very hard time."

"She's an alcoholic, isn't she?" Chelsea wasn't sure what made the words pop out of her mouth—perhaps an attempt to show him she understood what was going on, to show that she cared. She felt the need to have everything out in the open. There was too much happening right now to try to walk the precarious rope of secrecy.

His head snapped back to face her. "No!" His scowl was piercing. "You're completely mistaken!"

"I'm not condemning her, Jeff. I know alcoholism's a disease, something that needs to be treated. But it's pretty obvious that she drinks a lot. I don't think she can continue to hide it. She can't even walk straight."

His face had gone hard. "Her staggering has nothing to do with alcohol. It's ataxia."

"Ataxia?"

"A neuromuscular debility that's creating a problem with her gait. She has a severe weakness in her right leg, tingling in her hands and feet."

She stared up at him. "She's sick?"

"Yes, I'm afraid so. We don't know yet exactly what's causing it. The doctors are still doing tests."

"I'm sorry. I didn't realize—"

"She hid the symptoms for months. She didn't tell anyone, not even her personal physician. When it became obvious that something was wrong, she sent for me." He frowned. "Neuromuscular diseases aren't my specialty. There was nothing I could do but be with her, give her support and reassurance."

"Maybe that's what she needed most."

His expression softened. "She's a very brave woman, Chelsea. She's determined to face whatever it is with courage. She'd be furious if she knew I'd told you. She won't even let me call Brandon."

Chelsea was silent. She couldn't think of anything appropriate to say. She found his hand in the semi-darkness and squeezed it gently.

He squeezed back, and then suddenly he was holding her in his arms, pressing his face into her hair, drawing her tightly against him. It was a spontaneous, instinctive movement, and so was her kiss. "I won't tell anyone," she whispered. "I promise."

He closed his eyes and a long sigh came out of him. Then a loud moan from Lori brought them both to instant attention. They ran together to the main room.

The storm intensified along with Lori's labor. Lightning flashed and huge peals of thunder rolled overhead as Chelsea knelt beside the mattress and coached her sister through the painful contractions. Time slipped away, became irrelevant, as Lori panted and groaned through the dark morning. Chelsea was vaguely aware of Muriel's swaying movements through the room, knew that she had found a large pot and filled it with water and arranged somehow to hang it over the fire. Jeff was there too, checking Lori every few minutes, listening for the baby's heartbeat with his ear pressed to her distended abdomen, encouraging her gently. Periodically he raised the blanket that covered her legs and checked her cervix. Around noon, after a prolonged check, he gave Chelsea a meaningful glance.

"She's eight centimeters dilated now. Hang onto your hat."

A few minutes later Lori gave Jeff a wild-eyed look. "What's happening?" she gasped. Her legs started shaking and she gripped Chelsea's arm with fingers that felt like iron hooks. "I can't do it!" she cried. "I can't go on with this! Help me!" Fat drops of sweat stood out on her forehead.

Jeff took her hand. "It won't be much longer now, Lori. Everything's going fine. Just keep breathing."

"Where's Paul?" she cried, her face pinched in terror. "I want my husband!"

"He's not here right now." Jeff's voice was calm. "We're here to help you, Lori. You're going to be all right."

"I need some medication!" Lori moaned. "I can't take this pain!"

"Yes, you can." It was Muriel, who had managed to drag her chair close to the mattress. "You have to, for the baby. This is the hardest thing you'll ever do in your life, but you can do it. That's the secret of women's strength, Lori: looking pain in the face and going through it. It happens every time a woman gives birth."

Lori's eyes rolled toward her, and Chelsea turned to look at the older woman. Her face was set with a look of firm determination, but there was a softness around her eyes that betrayed a deep empathy with Lori's suffering. Chelsea reached over and touched Muriel's hand. Muriel's glance shifted toward her, and Chelsea smiled a silent thanks.

Jeff signaled for her to get Lori's attention as another strong contraction began to build. Chelsea felt her own forehead bead with sweat as she coached her sister in a clear, resolute voice. Lori groaned again, but this time didn't surrender to the pain. Muriel's words had strengthened something inside her, fortifying her for the effort ahead.

Chelsea held Lori's hand, guided her breathing, wiped the sweat off her forehead with a small dish towel. Through it all, she watched Jeff with growing admiration. He was in control of the whole situation; he seemed to know exactly what to say, what to do. If she'd been alone with Lori, she knew she'd have been crying and moaning too, probably running around the room in panic.

Finally, after what seemed an eternity, Jeff told Lori that she could start pushing. For the next hour Chelsea propped her sister's back with her arms while Lori strained to push the baby down the birth canal. Sweat ran off her face and soaked her tunic. No wonder they call it labor, Chelsea thought grimly. She'd never seen anyone work harder in her life.

Jeff knelt at the end of the mattress, encouraging Lori in a low, soothing voice. Between contractions, Lori collapsed back onto the mattress. She seemed to be almost asleep, and it was during one of these respites that Jeff signaled to Chelsea. He was frowning as he led her to the far end of the room.

"I'm afraid the baby's presenting posteriorly," he told her.

"What does that mean?"

"The head is turned the wrong way. The crown is pushing against her pubic bone. I'm going to have to turn it manually, if I can."

"Is she going to be all right?"

He nodded. "But it's going to hurt her. A lot. Maybe you want to go in another room while I try."

"No! I can't leave her at a time like this!"

He put his hand on her shoulder. "There's nothing you can do for her right now. Why don't you spare yourself?"

"I'm going to stay with her," she said resolutely. "She's my sister."

He nodded, squeezed her shoulder and quickly returned to Lori, who was starting to thrash on the mattress again.

"Give her this." Muriel's voice came from the shadows. Chelsea turned to find her standing by the door, holding something out to her.

"What is it?"

"A towel. For her to bite down on."

Chelsea went over to her and saw that what she was holding was indeed a towel that had been twisted tightly into a hard cord. "Isn't this kind of old-fashioned?"

"It's an old-fashioned delivery. We have to improvise." Muriel gave her a slight smile. "I remember my grandmother telling me how she used a knotted towel when my mother was born."

"Thanks." Chelsea took the towel and hurried

back to Lori, where Jeff was explaining to her in a clear voice what he was about to do.

Lori gave Chelsea a frightened look. "I'm not sure I'm going to be able to take this," she murmured.

"Sure you can." Chelsea forced a note of brightness into her voice. "You're my big sister. You've got to show me how it's done so I'll know what to do when it's my turn."

Lori groaned, but a half-smile curled the corners of her lips. Chelsea saw Jeff give her an approving nod as he knelt at the foot of the mattress.

"Here, put this between your teeth." Chelsea gave Lori the towel. "Bite down hard whenever it hurts."

"This is supposed to help the pain?"

"Trust me." Chelsea hoped Lori couldn't detect her own doubt, and was relieved when she took the towel in her mouth.

"Okay," said Jeff, "here we go."

Chelsea held out her hands for Lori to grasp and felt the fingers bite into her skin. Her sister's jaw worked fiercely against the towel, her face white with pain. She noticed that Jeff was sweating as he worked, his eyes dark and unfocused as he concentrated on maneuvering the baby inside the tight sheath of Lori's body. It seemed to take hours, though she knew it was probably only a matter of a few minutes, before he straightened. He was smiling so broadly that his dimple showed. Chelsea felt herself go suddenly weak all over.

"We did it" he announced. "We should have that baby out in the next five minutes. Give it your best, Lori."

Chelsea's heart pounded as Lori pushed through the next two contractions. She had never imagined that having a baby could be this exciting.

"Come on," Jeff coached. "Push . . . push . . . just a little more."

As Lori strained mightily, Chelsea closed her eyes and sent up a small prayer.

"Yes!" Jeff cried. "Great! That's wonderful."

Suddenly there was a thin cry. Chelsea looked up to see a wet, red-streaked baby squirming in Jeff's large hands.

"It's a boy!"

"Is he all right?" Lori asked anxiously.

"He's absolutely perfect." Jeff placed the baby on Lori's belly. The umbilical cord was still attached, a thick, blue rope, shining like silk. "And he looks full-term too. He's got plenty of body fat and he's certainly having no trouble breathing."

Tears jumped into Chelsea's eyes. She hugged Lori hard. "Congratulations, sis."

Lori looked up at her in wonder. "You mean it's over? It's really over?"

"Almost," said Jeff. "We have to wait for the placenta. Then I'll cut the cord and he's all yours."

Suddenly Lori was crying. "I wish Paul were here," she sobbed. "He wanted to be with me when the baby was born."

"You'll just have to give him another chance in a couple of years," Chelsea said.

Lori groaned.

Muriel came up to them. She handed Chelsea the clean bath towel. "This is to wrap him up in when the cord is cut."

"Me? You want me to wrap him?"

Muriel smiled. "I'll show you how it's done."

A few moments later Jeff tied the cord with string that Muriel had found in the knapsack and then cut it with a knife from the kitchen. Under Muriel's direction, Chelsea wrapped the infant securely in the towel, then handed him triumphantly to Lori.

"Go ahead and feed him," Muriel said. "Just put your nipple in his mouth. He'll know what to do." She lowered herself awkwardly to the floor and sat beside Lori, coaching her in a quiet voice.

Jeff stood up. His shirt was soaked with sweat and there were streaks of blood on his arms and hands. Chelsea quickly unknotted the towel Lori had used and handed it to him.

"Thanks." He breathed out a long sigh and grinned as he wiped the sweat and blood off. "Well, that certainly wasn't how I planned to spend my morning when I suggested a sail out to Eagle Island."

"Thank you *so* much." Chelsea felt tears pushing at her eyes again. "I don't know what would have happened if you hadn't been here. It's a miracle that you came."

"There is a miraculous element to our encounters, isn't there?"

She nodded, too exhausted and too euphoric to try and hide her profound agreement.

He dropped the towel on the floor and put his arm around her. "Come on, let's get some fresh air. I think the storm is over."

Chapter Eighteen

JEFF GUIDED HER OUT ONTO THE OPEN porch. The storm had passed, but dense fog had rolled in behind it, shrouding the island in thick, white mist. Chelsea could barely make out the sail-boat's mast.

"Oh no! We're fogged in!" She looked up at Jeff. "Stuart won't be able to get out here until it lifts."

"There's no rush. Lori and the baby are fine. Tell you what, though: I'll row out to the boat and radio the news in on the CB. That way your sister's husband will know he's a father."

"Thanks, Jeff. I'd really appreciate it."

"Why don't you come along? You can call Stuart and tell him what happened."

Moments later Chelsea was climbing aboard the sleek Winter sailboat. She gazed in awe at the polished wooden deck, the shining white gunwales. It was a far cry from the battered deck of *Chelsea's Choice*. Jeff led her down three steps and through a small door into the cabin. As on deck, everything was sleek and shining. Satiny wood paneling and plush blue and white upholstery screamed comfort and money. Jeff motioned for her to sit on a small couch while he stood at the counter and flipped a switch on the CB.

The box lit up and soon he was talking to a Coast Guard cutter out of Portland, asking them to relay a message to Paul LeBlanc. Then he turned the microphone over to Chelsea and she radioed *Chelsea's Choice.* Stuart answered right away, his heartwarming tone communicating his relief at hearing her voice. She explained what had happened and assured him that both she and Lori were fine.

"Jeff has offered to take us in when the fog lifts," she said. "But his engine isn't very big, so it will take a while."

"No way!" Stuart's voice crackled. "I want to see that you're safe and sound with my own eyes. I'll be there as soon as I can."

She signed off and turned to look at Jeff. He was leaning back on the couch, his eyes half closed. She felt a sudden, overwhelming wave of fatigue herself.

"Since we're safe, Stuart's not going to chance a run out to the island. And he doesn't want us going anywhere either. The fog is really thick. It may even last through the night."

Jeff opened his eyes to smile at her. "I can't say I'd object to spending the night with you. Maybe the fog is another one of those miracles."

Her stomach fluttered violently. She stood up. "I think I'd better get back and see how Lori's doing."

"She's probably sleeping by now." But he rose anyway, and as he did, his arm brushed hers. She felt the electric tingle all the way down to her toes. When she looked at his face, she saw that he'd experienced the same thing.

"Chelsea—"

She closed her eyes. "No," she whispered. "Don't." But her heart wasn't in her words; it was really crying for him to take her in his arms.

She didn't resist when he embraced her, or later, when he pulled her down onto the couch. He kissed her deeply and tenderly at first, then with growing passion. She melted against him, mindless, oblivious to everything but his presence, his firm body, his caressing hands, his clean, masculine scent. His fingers slid sensuously over her arms, slipped under her blouse, caressed her breasts. She lay wrapped in his strong arms, desire pulsing through her in waves. She had never even imagined that she could want a man so much. She didn't know that desire had the power to do this to a woman, that it could dissolve her, turn her into a furnace of passion. She felt as if she'd been changed into water and could flow and swirl anywhere. So when he suddenly pulled away from her and sat up, she let out a little cry.

"What's wrong? What is it?"

He bent his head into his hands. "I can't do this," he said hoarsely. "I promised you it wouldn't happen. I promised *myself.*" He got up and stood, gazing down at her for a long moment. "You are so beautiful," he whispered. "So incredibly beautiful."

Dazed, she sat up. "Jeff, I . . . I'm so confused. I don't understand what's happening to me." She struggled against the violent trembling that seized her. "Every time I see you . . ." She couldn't finish her sentence.

"I think it's obvious what's happening. And that we can't let it happen again." He turned and went to the door. "I'll wait for you on deck."

Chelsea fought tears as she adjusted her bra and tucked in her shirt. She was just overtired, she told herself. That was the real problem. She had been through too much, that was all. She'd be herself again when she got a good night's sleep. She wouldn't be subject to Jeff's wonderful smile or his sensual tenderness or his incredible kindness once she was rested.

She thought suddenly of Stuart, and a wave of self-hatred swept through her. How could she do this, when only minutes ago she'd been talking with the man she loved? Why did her body keep betraying her this way? She wiped angrily at a tear that escaped her left eye. When the fog lifted and Stuart came, she'd spend the night with him, show him how much she loved him. She thought of lying naked beside Stuart and something went numb inside her. He had been a good friend for so long; there had been so many years of familiar, comfortable companionship between them. How could their relationship ever turn passionate? Would she ever feel the melting ecstasy with Stuart that she'd just experienced in Jeff's arms? She felt suddenly sick to her stomach. She smoothed her blouse down over her breasts, slipped into her shoes and left the cabin.

The minute she stepped out on deck, she knew there was no chance of Stuart coming for them in the next few hours. The fog had thickened so much that the beach wasn't even visible. It was all she could do to make out Jeff, slouched on a gunwale in the stern. He rose as she came toward him, and without a word helped her into the little skiff that was bobbing beside the sailboat on the gray, mist-shrouded water.

As Jeff predicted, Lori was sleeping when they returned to the house. The baby was sleeping also, tucked down beside her, his tiny face cherubic in the firelight. Jeff stoked the fire while Chelsea gathered up and took the dirty towels into the kitchen, to wash them out in the antique copper sink.

It was a comfort to be alone with her thoughts as she worked. So much had happened in the last few hours, it felt as if the whole world had turned upside down and started rotating backward. It was all she could do to get her bearings, to remind herself that it was natural to feel so disturbed; witnessing a birth stirred up a lot of emotions. The intensity of her feelings for Jeff were only temporary. They didn't mean anything. But she couldn't stop thinking about the way he had held her in his arms, the tenderness in his eyes as he'd told her she was beautiful. She wanted to experience it again, to lie under his gaze, to feel the rich flush of joy that had suffused her.

She rinsed the towels, wrung them out, and spread them on the counter to dry. She was wondering what other task she could do to keep herself busy, when Muriel entered the kitchen.

"I'd like to talk to you," she said.

"Sure." Chelsea felt an affectionate warmth toward the older woman now. She had been so supportive during Lori's labor and delivery, and she'd also helped Lori adjust to breast-feeding immediately after the baby's birth. "Why don't we go sit down?"

Muriel shook her head and leaned against a tall cabinet. "Here would be better. I'd prefer to speak where I know we won't be disturbed."

"Okay."

"It's about Jefferson's behavior toward you."

The hairs on the back of Chelsea's neck lifted. "I think you've already told me how you feel about that."

"I want you to understand, it's nothing personal.

It's simply that he has a very large inheritance coming to him. In the near future, it will demand his utmost attention. People in our situation are often forced to make some very unpleasant choices."

"I don't know anything about Jeff's choices, Mrs. Winter. Those are up to him."

"No, my dear, they're not. That's what I'm trying to explain to you. In our social station, most of our choices are dictated by outside considerations."

"Such as where to live and whom to marry?"

"Exactly."

Chelsea lifted her chin. "I don't pretend to understand your world, Mrs. Winter. But perhaps you should stop assuming you understand mine. I'm not after your son's money or his social status, or anything else. I'm not after him at all. I'm proud of my work; I love my job; I'm engaged to a wonderful man. And I happen to like being who I am: just plain old Chelsea Adams."

Muriel raised a doubtful eyebrow. "Are you denying you are infatuated with my son?"

"I admire Jeff; I like him; I think he's a wonderful doctor, but . . ." For some reason, she couldn't complete the sentence.

"You see, my dear, you've proved my point. You can't deny that you are attracted to him."

"That doesn't mean I'm after him."

"Perhaps not, but he is clearly interested in you. Let me be frank. Jefferson cannot afford an unfortunate liaison at this point in his life. Anymore than he can afford to continue this doctor whim of his. The time has come for him to assume his rightful place in the world. He will soon be swamped with investments, stock portfolios, financial management."

"He's not going back to Africa with Project HOPE?"

"Africa? Of course not. That's hardly an appropriate enterprise for him, hiding himself away in the jungle like that. He's much too important. Besides, he simply can't afford the time."

"Can't afford time for what?" Jeff stepped into the kitchen.

"Oh, Jefferson! You startled me!" Muriel drew back against the cabinet.

"I'd like to know what you were talking about."

"Nothing, dear. Simply a little inconsequential chat."

"Enlighten me."

"Well, if you must know, I was discussing your future with Chelsea."

"My future?"

"Yes, I was telling her about the overwhelming responsibilities that go with your inheritance. I was explaining why you won't have time to return to Africa—"

He cut her off. "I've told you before that I won't allow some archaic notion of class obligation to dictate my behavior. I thought I'd made that clear."

"So you have, Jefferson. But you're so young yet, you don't understand—"

"I'm thirty-two years old. I've been making my own decisions, living my own life, for fifteen years. I don't intend to change simply because I came back to the States to visit you."

"Jefferson—"

"And one more thing: my relationship with Chelsea has nothing to do with you. Whatever bond she and I choose to cultivate, now or in the future, is our business. Not yours."

Chelsea watched Muriel stiffen. "Jefferson, if you think you can treat me this way and get away with it, you are seriously mistaken. I advise you to remember that I have full control of your inheritance. I can and will cut you off if you disregard me."

Jeff stared at her for a long, tense moment, then turned on his heel and left.

When Muriel looked back at Chelsea, she was smiling. "You see, my dear, everyone, even my rebellious Jefferson, can be brought to reason."

Nausea climbed Chelsea's throat as she retreated to the sanctuary of the main room, where the baby was waking up in Lori's arms. There was no sign of Jeff at all.

Chelsea and Muriel ate in silence while Lori nursed the baby. No one spoke of Jeff's absence. Lori seemed to sense that something had happened, but she was too absorbed by the baby to ask questions. When they finished eating, Muriel announced that she was going to lie down upstairs. She climbed the steps haltingly, gripping the rail in her hand, and Chelsea felt a wave of pity for the woman. It must be extremely hard for someone who was so bent on control over her family members to be losing control of her own body. Chelsea glanced at Lori. "I think I'll go take a walk, if you don't mind being alone for a little while."

"Alone?" Lori didn't lift her gaze from the baby's face. "Who's alone?"

The fog had lifted slightly. Chelsea could make out the sailboat riding the lazy ocean swells in the little cove. It didn't look like they'd have to spend the night on the island after all. The sun would break through the fog soon, and Stuart would be heading out to the island to meet her. Chelsea felt a wave of relief, oddly mixed with resignation. She walked down to the beach, stooping to pick up an occasional stone or shell. She wondered where Jeff had gone.

She climbed onto the boulder where Stuart had proposed, sat and curled her arms around her knees, gazing out to sea. She felt exhausted and exhilarated at the same time. She was an aunt now; she had a nephew, and it made her think about having her own children. What would they look like? Would their births be easier than the one she had just witnessed?

She heard a sound behind her and turned to see Jeff descending the path from the trees beyond the house. He had his hands in his pockets; his head was bent forward; there was a grave expression on his handsome face. She wondered if he would speak to her after the humiliating confrontation with his mother.

A moment later he spotted her and waved. She noted the little flutter of pleasure in her chest as he came toward her.

"I'm glad I found you alone," he said, climbing up beside her.

As she slid over on the boulder to make room for him, he dropped something into her hand. "A present for you." It was a tiny scallop shell, perfectly fluted and pure white, with a small hole at its apex.

"Thank you, Jeff. What's the occasion?"

"It's sort of an apology for my mother's behavior. It was unforgivable."

"You don't need to apologize to me. I know she was just defending you because she loves you."

He gave her a long look. "That's very perceptive

of you. Most people can't see beneath her tyrannical exterior. The fact is, she's terrified right now."

"Terrified?"

He nodded. "Of losing me, of losing control of her body. I think it takes incredible courage for her just to get out of bed in the morning. She needs to know that someone understands her, accepts her the way she is." He sighed. "I'm just having a very hard time doing that right now."

"I'm sorry if I created the situation that caused your quarrel."

"You didn't create the situation, Chelsea. It was her own doing. All that talk about social class and inheritance turns my stomach, but it's the only life she's ever known."

"But she's right, social class *does* make a big difference in people's lives. I'll never have the kind of future you have. I'll never have your social obligations. I'm not cultured or educated. I don't have breeding."

He looked at her. "What you have, Chelsea, is something no amount of money or upbringing could ever give. You're bright and alive and filled with spirit. Those qualities are more precious than any medical degree or family legacy."

Chelsea gazed down at the little shell in her hand. Her eyes stung and her throat felt strangely full. "Maybe we're each given the things we need for our own particular lives."

He nodded silently and stared out to sea. He was quiet for a long time. The water slowly climbed the beach; the tide was coming in. A gull swooped and landed a few feet from the boulder and regarded them with a shrewd, orange-ringed eye. Finally, Jeff spoke in a low voice.

"She asks so much of me. She always has. It's one of the reasons I went to Africa: to get away, to give myself some space to think, to make my own choices without her interference."

"And then she got sick and you came back."

"I had no choice."

Chelsea stared at the little sailboat, rocking gently on the water. It was hard to believe that something so small and fragile-looking could have survived the storm that just passed over the island. Yet it looked untouched, exactly as it had before the storm: elegant and sleek, lying gracefully on the gray water. Its strength lay in its ability to ride on top of the waves, not to submit to the weather's whims.

"We always have choices, even when we don't recognize them," she said quietly. "Sometimes we just need something or someone to open our eyes."

He looked at her closely. "What are you saying?"

"I guess I'm trying to say that you can't always accommodate the wishes of the people you love. Even though you might want to more than anything in the world. Sometimes you just have to be true to your own dreams in life, whatever they are. If you live by chasing someone else's dream, it's not really your life anymore, is it?"

"You're saying I should give up my inheritance and go back to Africa."

"I'm saying you have to give yourself that choice."

"It's not that simple," he said softly. "Though I wish to God it were."

They sat for another long interval in silence. Chelsea noticed that small patches of sun were flecking the water. She lifted her arms slowly to massage the back of her neck. "I can't believe everything that's happened today. I'm afraid I just can't absorb it all:

being stranded here, the baby's birth, your mother's illness."

"Give it time," he said gently. " 'Time is man's angel.' "

"I like that. Another one of your quotes?"

"Von Schiller. Pretty obscure, but one of my personal favorites. It's helped me through a lot of rough spots." He reached to take her hand. The gesture seemed so natural and appropriate to the moment, she didn't even consider its implications. They sat side by side in the growing sunlight, watching the play of light on the waves.

The fog had disappeared completely by four o'clock that afternoon, leaving a clear blue sky in its wake. Chelsea watched for *Chelsea's Choice* from the porch, while Jeff checked on Lori and the baby. When the boat finally came chugging into the cove, she ran down to the beach, waving both arms excitedly. She could see both Stuart and Paul waving from the deck. She was glad Stuart had thought to bring Paul; Lori's husband was extremely protective and would need to see for himself that Lori and the baby were all right.

They came quickly into shore in an inflatable raft, and Chelsea greeted them both with enthusiastic hugs, then led them to the house. Lori was still lying on the mattress, propped up on a collection of pillows and blankets that Muriel had found; she was holding the baby in the crook of her left arm, gazing down at him tenderly. The fire had warmed the room, and the gentle glow of the firelight was playing over Lori's beautiful face. When she looked up and saw Paul, she gave a little cry of delight.

"Let's leave them alone for a few minutes," Jeff

suggested, helping Muriel to her feet and guiding her out onto the porch. Chelsea followed with Stuart, who looped an arm possessively around her shoulder.

"You won't believe how worried I was," he told her. "When that storm broke, I called the Coast Guard to find out if it would be safe to make a run for it, and they told me to stay put. I felt so helpless! All I could do was pray you two would be okay. Of course, if I'd known Lori was in labor, I'd have come anyway."

"We were fine, thanks to Jeff," Chelsea assured him.

"Well, I guess I can't hate the guy then, can I?" His hand still around her shoulder, he steered her over to where Jeff and Muriel were seated. "Hey, Jeff, thanks a lot for everything." He held out his hand. "Looks like you saved the day around here. Wish there was some way I could repay you."

Jeff smiled. "No need, my friend. Delivering a baby safely is its own reward."

"Well, I want you to know how much Chelsea and I appreciate it. That baby is about to become my nephew, you know." He squeezed Chelsea a little tighter against his side. "Tell you what, why don't you come to our wedding? Two o'clock on Sunday, the twenty-third. It's not going to be anything fancy, but there'll be good food, I guarantee. There always is when Chels is around."

Jeff frowned. "I'm not at all sure—"

"No, we insist. Don't we, Chels?"

Chelsea cringed inwardly. Stuart was grinning broadly, proud of his burst of inspiration. He obviously thought he was doing Jeff a huge favor by inviting him to the wedding. "Sure," she said weakly, unable to meet Jeff's eyes. "We'd love to have both you and your mother come."

"Well, thanks for the invitation. We'll certainly consider it."

She knew he was looking at her and that she couldn't keep her face averted any longer. His gaze drew her, forced her eyes upward. She felt her heart clench as her eyes met his. For she saw something there she'd never seen before: a stark, open pain. A pain that mirrored her own.

Chapter Nineteen

STUART OPENED THE *CHELSEA*'S THROTtle all the way up on the trip back to the mainland, and by seven o'clock Lori and the baby were resting comfortably in the maternity wing of the Maine Medical Center. Chelsea called her mother and told her the good news.

"It turns out that Lori's doctor miscalculated her due date by almost three weeks. The baby's not premature at all. He's almost eight pounds."

"Who does he look like?"

"Himself. He's really cute. Light hair, a sweet little chin. I think he might have Paul's nose. They're naming him Andrew Jefferson. Andrew after Dad."

"Where did they get the Jefferson?"

Chelsea laughed. "It's a long story, Mom. I'll let Lori explain the whole thing when you see her." She hung up, grinning, and went back down the hall to Lori's room.

Stuart was deep in a Red Sox conversation with Paul, so Chelsea sat with Lori for a while and they admired the baby together.

"How do you feel?"

"Wonderful. Thrilled." Lori grinned and patted her stomach. "A little empty, though."

"That must be a relief."

"It sure is."

"Do you think you'll be back on your feet for the wedding? I want you there as my matron of honor."

"Don't worry, Chels. I'll be ready. If you are."

Chelsea frowned. "Don't start, sis."

Lori shook her head. "I just want you to be really sure."

"I am."

"When is Holly coming?"

"I'm not sure of the exact day. I haven't had a chance to talk with her; we keep communicating by answering machine." Chelsea was suddenly aware of a strange, empty feeling herself. As if something had just been snatched away from her. "Things have been just a little too crazy lately." She forced a laugh.

"That's an understatement," Lori replied.

"I'll call her tonight. I want to tell her about my new nephew."

"Say hi for me." Lori yawned widely and smiled down at the baby.

"We should let you get some sleep." Chelsea glanced at Stuart. "How about if you guys put a lid on the baseball talk? Lori needs her rest."

It was dark when Stuart took Chelsea back to his house to pick up her car.

"I'm totally wiped," she said, slumping back in the truck seat as he pulled up in front of his cabin. The halogen light mounted on his roof lit the inside of the truck with a purple tinge. "Bed is going to feel unbelievably good tonight."

He slid over next to her and put his arm around

her. "After what happened this morning, I don't want to let you out of my sight. Why don't you stay the night? We *are* engaged, after all." He drew her closer, nuzzled her cheek. "What do you say, Chels? Isn't it time we slept together?"

She smiled into his eyes, which were too close to bring into focus. "Actually, I was thinking the same thing this afternoon. I just hope you won't feel insulted if I fall asleep in the middle of things. I'm so tired tonight, I can hardly keep my eyes open."

"Hey, we don't have to *do* anything. Just be together. Hold each other through the night."

"Sounds nice," Chelsea murmured. She closed her eyes and concentrated on the sensation of Stuart's lips on hers. They were warm and pleasantly soft. She pressed closer, so that she could experience the hardness of his teeth, draw the musk of his breath into her lungs. She felt so sheltered and safe in his arms. There was no one in the world with whom she felt more secure. Stuart was the man she loved, the man with whom she was going to spend the rest of her life. She waited expectantly for a yearning throb of arousal. But there was nothing.

It was just fatigue, she told herself as Stuart's kisses moved from her mouth to her neck, and his fingers opened the top two buttons of her blouse. She heard him whisper her name as he slid his hand inside her bra to cup her breast. She waited for the erotic shock to startle her, the way it had when Jeff had touched her. But again there was nothing. Only the familiar comfort of Stuart's hand.

Tears of frustration stung her eyes. What was wrong with her? Why couldn't she feel passion for Stuart? He was the nicest man in the world. She tried again to summon the arousal she longed for, concentrating all her will on the effort. But her body would not respond. And deep within, a voice told her that the reason had nothing to do with her fatigue. It was something far more profound, something that would have far-reaching and harmful consequences in their marriage. The critical element of passion was missing. And, try as she might to invoke it, it would never be there. She and Stuart had a deep and abiding friendship, but that was all the relationship would ever be.

Suddenly, she remembered the words she'd spoken to Jeff on the beach at Eagle Island. She could almost hear them as Stuart's lips claimed hers once again. *You can't always accommodate the wishes of the people you love. Even though you might want to more than anything in the world. Sometimes you just have to be true to your own dreams.* She realized with a shock that the words applied to her, perhaps even more than they applied to Jeff. Because the reason she'd accepted Stuart's proposal didn't have anything to do with her own dreams. It had to do with her fondness for him, her desire to please this man who had been her dear friend for so many years. She placed her hands on Stuart's chest and gently drew away.

"What's wrong?" He was frowning in bewilderment.

She touched his cheek. "Stuart," she said in a choked voice. "I'm so sorry. But I can't go through with the wedding."

"What! Why not?"

"I just can't."

His frown deepened toward pain. "I don't understand."

"It's not you, Stuart. You're a wonderful, sensitive man. It's me. It's just not right for me."

He did exactly what she dreaded, what she prayed he wouldn't do; his eyes filled with tears and he buried his face in his hands.

She put her hand on his arm. "Please don't. I know this seems cruel, and you probably think I'm being very unkind, but I don't know what else to do, Stuart. It would be worse if I married you when I don't . . ." She couldn't finish.

He lifted his head to look at her. "When you don't love me?"

"No." She shook her head. "I do love you. Very much. But I love you like a friend. Like a brother. Not the way a wife should love a husband."

He was silent for a long time. When he finally spoke, his voice was sad, muffled as if by distance. "I kept hoping that something would change. When you agreed to get married, I thought maybe it had."

"I wish it had, Stuart. I wish to God it had. I can't *bear* the thought of hurting you." Her eyes filled with tears. "I'm so sorry."

There was a long silence. They sat motionless in the dimly lit truck cab.

"When did you figure all this out?" Stuart asked softly.

"Just now. But I think it's been coming for the past couple of weeks."

"Since you met Jeff Blaine." It was a statement, not a question. She didn't answer.

After a while he gave a low, sad chuckle. "You know, it's funny, but I sensed something when I first met him, that day I walked in and he was treating your knee. It was like there was an electric current flowing between you. I felt left out, excluded."

"I'm sorry, Stuart. Honestly."

"You shouldn't apologize for your feelings. Besides, if you and he—"

"No, it's nothing like that! I'm not breaking our engagement because of Jeff! He's not even available. At least not to me. His mother doesn't approve of me, and he's very restricted by his social class. Please don't think my feelings have anything to do with him!"

"It wouldn't matter if they did," he said quietly. "The end result is still the same." He paused. "I think I must have known unconsciously that this was coming. For some reason, I don't really feel surprised."

"I'm so sorry, Stuart," she whispered. "If there was any way on earth I could change my feelings, I'd do it in a minute."

"I know," he said gently. "And I'll be all right. It'll just take me a little while." He hesitated and gave her a half smile. "It doesn't make sense, but what feels worst right now is knowing that my father won't get his wish. He was really looking forward to our wedding." His voice caught. "I can't help thinking that the wedding would have been his last opportunity to see everybody together. The whole family was planning to come. All of his brothers and sisters. Even his cousin from Chicago, the one he fished with as a boy."

She put her arms around him, and they embraced for a long time in silence. Leafy shadows from the moonlit windshield swayed over the dashboard. Stars glimmered overhead. In the distance Chelsea could hear the soothing lap of water against the shore.

"I have an idea," she said finally. "What if we go ahead with the plans? Keep the date and the time and everything, only instead of our wedding, we'll make it a get-well party for your father."

"A get-well party?"

She nodded. "We'll invite all the same people, just tell them to bring a get-well gift instead of a wedding present." She felt the pain in the center of her chest ease slightly. "It could work, Stuart. It might even help your father recover. They say sometimes that love and laughter are the best medicines."

His expression was curious, attentive. "That's not a bad idea."

"It's a *great* idea, even if I did think of it myself!" Chelsea grinned. "We'll invite everybody he knows. We'll invite the whole town!"

Stuart laughed. "God, Chels, you're wonderful. If you're not going to marry me, at least you have to promise me that we'll still see each other and still go out on *Chelsea's Choice* from time to time."

"Are you kidding? You know I love that boat as much as you do." She hugged him again. "Don't worry, Stuart. I'll never stop being your friend, no matter what happens."

She called Holly as soon as she got home and told her the change in plans. "But promise me you'll still come," she said. "This get-well party is going to be the biggest Maynard Landing's seen in a long time."

"I wouldn't miss it for the world!" Holly sounded uncharacteristically cheerful. It struck Chelsea that she hadn't heard that particular tone in her friend's voice in over two years.

"Something's happened, hasn't it? You sound different."

Holly giggled. "I know I should have written, but

I've been awfully busy." Her voice lowered to a confiding murmur. "I've met somebody, Chels."

"A man?"

"Very definitely."

"Well, don't keep me in suspense."

"His name is Martin Rodriguez. He's the head chef at the Hilton out here. He's not as good-looking as Brandon, but he's a lot more open and honest. Actually, he kind of reminds me of Stuart. Sensitive, kind, funny; everything I ever wanted. He's amazing, Chels."

"You're going to have to bring me a picture when you come."

"I can do even better than that. I was hoping you wouldn't mind if I brought him along."

"That would be wonderful! I'm dying to meet him!"

After another half hour of joyful conversation, Chelsea reluctantly hung up. Holly had agreed to come for the whole week, and both she and Martin would help with the food preparation. She would arrive on the Friday before the party. Chelsea was so happy that she did a wild dance around the living room. As she swooped and twirled past her desk, something fell out of her pocket. She looked down and saw the small white shell Jeff had given her.

She picked it up, cupping it in her hand. It seemed to glow there, shining in the semidarkness. He had said it was a present, and she'd known he was half joking, but now, gazing down at the delicate shell, she realized that it was indeed a gift, one of the most precious she'd ever received.

She took it into her bedroom, located a long gold chain in her jewelry box, and threaded it through the little hole in the shell. As she hung it around her neck, tears filled her eyes. She thought of how Jeff had been forced to yield his dreams to the exhausting demands of his mother, of how he had bent his will repeatedly to her need. It was all because he loved her, she knew. But what kind of love was it that killed a person's dreams?

The two weeks following the baby's birth were a whirlwind of activity. Chelsea visited Lori and her new nephew every day, and spent her free time throwing herself into preparations for Dan Potter's get-well party. The list of guests grew daily, until, at 150 Chelsea insisted that Stuart stop calling people.

"I've never handled more than sixty on my own," she told him on the phone one warm afternoon. "I'm already going out of my mind, and it's only Tuesday!"

"I thought your mother said she'd help fill in for Lori."

"She did, but she's next to useless in the kitchen. She doesn't know anything about how Strawberry Lace works. I still have to do most of the baking. Holly's not coming until Friday."

"Let me help, then."

"You're going to have to, Stuart. I can't imagine getting along without you."

Friday dawned sunny and warm, a perfect June morning. Chelsea spent the morning making paté and petits fours for Sunday afternoon's party. Then she dressed in her best blue linen slacks and matching flowered blouse, and drove to Portland, stopping in at Lori's house on the way to check on how her sister was coping after her return from the hospital. She held Andrew for a few minutes, rocking him in her arms, fascinated by the steady gaze in his slate-colored eyes.

"I think his eyes are definitely going to be blue," Lori said. "See how they're getting lighter around the pupils?"

Chelsea couldn't detect any change, but was happy to agree anyway. "Of course he'll have blue eyes! He's your son, Lori!"

"Paul's too. Don't you think his ears look just like his father's?"

"If you say so. You know them a lot better than I do."

Lori laughed. "Wait until you have a baby, Chelsea. You'll be acting just as crazy as I am."

"I don't think that's going to be any time soon." She looked at her sister wistfully. "Maybe I shouldn't have broken things off with Stuart."

"Don't even *think* that way! I've told you all along, as wonderful as Stuart is, he's not the right guy for you to marry."

"I guess I have to admit you were right, for once."

"For *once!* Chels, you know God made me your big sister for a darn good reason: to keep you out of trouble."

Both women were giggling hysterically by the time Chelsea left for the airport to pick up Holly.

Holly's flight was right on time, but at first Chelsea thought her friend had missed the flight. It wasn't until the sleek, stylishly-dressed dark-haired woman took off her sunglasses that Chelsea identified her.

"Holly!" she squealed. "I didn't even recognize you!"

The two women embraced warmly. "I brought Martin," Holly announced, pulling away and motioning to a short, balding man with a dark mustache who came toward them, grinning broadly. Chelsea shook his hand happily and was amused to note Holly's insistence on sitting in the backseat with him while Chelsea drove back to her apartment. Their conversation was intense, almost urgent, as they tried to catch up on the past year and a half since they'd seen each other. At the apartment, Chelsea settled them into the spare bedroom, then took them downstairs to the shop and put them to work.

She was pleased with how easily Martin adapted to the Strawberry Lace kitchen, and gratified by his many compliments on the recipes they would be using. She drew Holly aside to congratulate her on her good fortune.

"He's wonderful!" she said. "Don't let him get away, whatever you do!"

"Don't worry, I don't intend to." Holly grinned broadly. "What seems so weird to me now is that I ever thought I was in love with Brandon Winter. Martin's an absolute prince compared to Brandon!"

"That reminds, me: I've still got Brandon's ring. Don't let me forget to give it to you. You can probably sell it to finance a new car or something."

Holly laughed. "That's not a bad idea. How are things going with *you,* manwise?"

"Same as always. You know me."

Holly's face sobered. "Yes, I do know you, Chelsea. And I don't think you're telling me the whole truth. There's something about you that's different, that's more radiant than I've ever seen you before. If I didn't know better, I'd think you were in love."

Chelsea felt the color rush to her cheeks.

"Come on," Holly said. "Tell me who he is."

"You're not going to believe me if I do."

"Try me."

"His name's Jeff Blaine. He's Brandon's half brother."

Holly's eyes widened. "Jeff? You're kidding! I remember Brandon talking about him. Jeff was the black sheep of the family—he ran off to Africa and drove Muriel crazy. I always wished Brandon had his spirit. He came back?"

Chelsea nodded.

"So how long have you two been seeing each other?"

"We haven't. I mean, we've *seen* each other, but that's about all. Anyway, it doesn't matter. Muriel's dead set against me, so nothing's going to come of it."

Holly nodded sympathetically. "You don't have to tell me how Muriel Winter operates. She's probably getting a couple of Boston debutantes lined up right now for her sons. You're smart to put him out of your mind."

But despite all her assertions, Chelsea found that she couldn't stop thinking about Jeff. All afternoon, as she worked industriously, making crabmeat stuffing for the mushrooms, mixing liver and chicken paté, creating vats of spreads and dips, she felt her cheeks glowing with a sweet, heady mixture of excitement and desire.

Sunday's weather was perfect. Chelsea went out to Stuart's place early to set up and make sure everything would be ready by two, when the guests were due to arrive. Holly and Martin were going to church before they joined her at Stuart's, but they assured her they would be there well before the party began.

Stuart gave her a doubtful look when she got out of the van.

"You can't wear the Strawberry Lace outfit to this!" he complained. "You're a guest today too."

"Well, what do you suggest?"

"I don't know. Don't you have a new summer dress or something?"

"Only the white one I bought for the wedding."

"Wear that," he said. "You look great in it."

"Won't it hurt your feelings?"

"Of course not." He squeezed her shoulder. "To be honest, once I started thinking about it, I realized you were right. I've always just assumed we'd get married, so I never even looked around until now." She was startled to see a slight blush mount his neck.

"You're seeing somebody, aren't you?"

He shrugged. "Sort of. I've taken Melanie Bonneau out a couple of times."

Chelsea laughed. "In just this past week? You didn't waste any time, did you?"

He grinned sheepishly.

"That's great! I'm really happy for you. Is she coming to the party today?"

He nodded. "I didn't think you'd mind."

"I don't. In fact, it makes this a lot easier for me." She slipped the tiny engagement ring off her finger and handed it to him as she stood on tiptoe to kiss his cheek. "Thanks for everything," she whispered.

He smiled down at her. "You keep it."

"No. It doesn't belong to me anymore."

"Yes it does, Chels. It will always belong to you." He slipped it quickly onto her right hand. "There," he said happily. "Now it's a friendship ring."

She put both arms around him and hugged him tightly. "I'm so lucky have you for a friend, Stuart. Sometimes I think I'm the luckiest woman in the world."

Chapter Twenty

BEHIND THE CABIN, CHELSEA LAID sheets over a makeshift table Stuart had rigged from sawhorses and a sheet of plywood. Stacks of lobster traps made a wall between the table and the grill, while a section of fence that Stuart had decorated with old lobster buoys screened the view of the driveway and the road beyond. Stuart scattered folding chairs around the yard in conversation-sized clusters and brought out his rocking chair as the seat of honor for his father. In the tiny kitchen, Chelsea spread paté on cucumber slices and toast squares. She steamed clams in the big, black pot that Stuart kept under the sink, and stirred the dressing into the potato salad. The lobsters, moving around lazily in a tub of seawater on the kitchen floor, wouldn't be cooked until the guests started arriving. The corn could be roasted right in the husk over hot coals in Stuart's grill outside.

By noon everything that could be done ahead of time was ready. Chelsea stood for a moment, surveying her work with satisfaction. "I think it'll be a great party," she told Stuart as he came through the kitchen. "I'm done until people start coming."

"Go home and change into that dress," he urged her. "I'll start the coffee."

"Not before one-thirty."

"Coffee's one thing I can make," he growled. "Now get going."

Chelsea found herself relishing the weather as she drove back to her apartment. It was the perfect day for a party, the kind of day a June bride would probably kill for. She felt a strange tingle in the small of her back. It could have been her wedding day. It would have been, if she hadn't realized how important making choices really was.

She let herself into the apartment, changed out of the Strawberry Lace outfit and into the white summer dress that she'd picked out to serve as a wedding gown. It was simple and attractive, with a scoop neck, lace-trimmed bodice, cap sleeves, and a full skirt that fell from the fitted waist. She eyed herself critically in the mirror. Lori had been right: it wasn't a wedding dress, really. Just a pretty little summer outfit. She thought again of the beautiful bridal gown in the shop in Portland. Her dream gown. She wondered if it was still on layaway. Probably Lori had been too busy to even think about it. She'd have to call the shop and ask them to put it back on display. She no longer even had an excuse to look at it, not to mention buy it.

She piled her hair on top of her head, studied the effect, then brushed it out again so that it hung over her shoulders in long red-gold strands. She eyed the hat on the top shelf of her closet. It was a wide-brimmed, white straw hat that she'd purchased instead of a bridal veil and crown. She slid it off the shelf and placed it on her head. Perfect. It set off her hair and face beautifully, just as it had in the shop. She smiled at her reflection. She'd wear it to the party. There was nothing obviously bridal about it, after all; those associations had just been in her own mind. And the hat had the added advantage of keeping the sun off her face and preventing a sunburn.

When Chelsea pulled into Stuart's driveway a half hour later, she saw that several people had already arrived. Lori's car was there, as well as the Saturn that Holly and Martin had rented.

She found everyone out back, setting out finger food on long trays at the table. Holly was the first to spot her. "You look fantastic!"

"Thanks." Chelsea started taking curried chicken hors d'oeuvres out of a box and placing them on trays.

"No, you don't!" Lori warned. "You look too pretty to do that. Besides, you've already done more than your share."

"That's right," Holly and Stuart chorused. "Go sit down and let us finish this."

Chelsea protested, but her friends remained adamant. She finally retreated to a lawn chair and sat there for a few minutes, watching the play of sunlight on the calm water of the cove and fingering the little shell around her neck. There were several sailboats in the distance, one closer in, sailing near the mouth of the cove.

Stuart came up behind her. "Hope she's got a low keel," he commented. "Or she'll run aground on that sandbar."

Chelsea watched as the boat slid through the neck

of the cove. She thought it looked vaguely familiar, but then all sailboats looked alike to her.

A sudden wail from Holly brought her to her feet. "We forgot the flowers!"

"Oh no!" Lori cried. "And none of the shops are open today either. Damn!" She was shifting back and forth from one leg to the other, rocking Andrew, who was strapped to her chest in a soft cotton pouch.

"I'll go get some wild ones," Chelsea offered. She started down the sloping lawn toward the water's edge. Stuart only mowed a small section of his yard; the rest he let run to meadow, where hundreds of daisies and buttercups bobbed in the sunlight.

She loved wildflowers; they had always been her favorites, and she relished the sheer pleasure of building the bouquet in her arms. She wandered through the tall grass, enjoying the way it brushed against the folds of her skirt as she bent and picked. She found not only daisies and buttercups, but cornflowers, wild hyacinths, and, in the shade of the trees down closer to the water, a bed of fragrant lilies of the valley. She moved out of sight of the cabin, following the flowers as if they were a trail, focusing all her attention on creating a huge, brilliant bouquet.

She didn't pay attention to the outboard motor at first; it was just background noise, a sound she'd heard thousands of times in her life, no more arresting than an auto engine. She didn't even lift her head at the sound of a boat hull scraping stones. It wasn't until she heard the low drumbeat of running footsteps that she straightened and turned. A small skiff had been beached a few hundred yards from where she stood, and a man was running up the sloping meadow toward her.

She didn't recognize him for a moment; the glimmer of sunlight off the water was too bright. But when he moved into the shade of the pines where she'd found the lilies of the valley, she let out a gasp of recognition.

It was Jeff Blaine. Her heart banged eagerly against her rib cage as she lifted her arm to wave to him. Then she saw that his expression wasn't the grin she'd first thought, but a dark scowl.

"What's wrong?" she called as he came closer. Part of her wanted to laugh, she was so happy to see him.

He didn't answer, but was suddenly beside her, grabbing her upper arm in a viselike fist.

"Don't try to get away," he warned her. "It won't do any good." He started pulling her back toward the skiff.

"Jeff? What are you doing?"

He clapped his free hand abruptly over her mouth. "Quiet!"

Instinctively, she struggled to free herself. But instead of releasing her, Jeff swung around, lifted her in his arms and heaved her over his shoulder. Then he continued down the meadow to the boat.

She was so stunned that she didn't even think to scream. She was vaguely aware that her hat had sailed off and disappeared in the tall grass. She felt the heave of his shoulder against her pelvis and heard the pound of his footsteps as he ran. It wasn't until he had tumbled her into the boat, pushed off, and was gunning the outboard, that her brain collected itself enough to try and make sense of what was happening.

"Jeff!" She tried to yell above the roar of the outboard. She saw that they were heading toward the sailboat she'd seen earlier, which was moored in the middle of the cove. "What's going on? What are you doing?" She lifted her arm to shade her eyes, to make out his expression against the glare of light.

"Don't try to talk me out of it," he yelled back at her. "I'm not changing my mind."

"Changing your mind about what?"

"I'll explain when we get on board."

She didn't ask any more questions. A moment later he was tying the skiff to the sailboat's stern and pulling her aboard. He ducked into the pilothouse to start the engine and swing the boat around. Apparently he didn't want to waste time waiting for the big sail to catch the wind.

Chelsea followed him into the pilothouse. "Do you mind explaining what you're doing?"

"Sit down." He pointed to a deck chair. "Don't talk."

She did as he said, aware that great waves of adrenaline were coursing through her body. It wasn't fear either; she didn't believe he would hurt her. She was more excited than anything else. Just being near him again made her whole body come alive. And whatever he was doing, for whatever reason, was certainly thrilling. It was like being in her own private adventure movie.

As soon as the boat cleared the neck of the cove, he cut the engine and turned to face her. "I know this may seem cruel, but it's necessary, Chelsea."

"What's necessary?"

"I had to get you out of there. I couldn't wait any longer." He pushed his hands down into his pockets. "Believe me, I tried. I spent the last two weeks trying to get you out of my mind, trying to tell myself that what you do with your life isn't any of my business, that you can get married to whomever you want. I know that's what I'm supposed to feel, that it doesn't make any sense for me not to be able to reconcile myself to your marriage—"

"Marriage?"

"Please. Let me finish. The fact is, the more I told myself to stay out of it, the more I knew I had to do something. The more I tried to convince myself that it wasn't my business, the more I realized it *was.*" He leaned toward her. "I know you're probably very, very angry with me right now. And I know I'm probably destroying whatever chance I might ever have had with you, but I couldn't just stand by and watch you get married and see my whole future go down the drain. Not without at least laying my cards on the table."

Chelsea stared at him in confusion. Then, suddenly, everything clicked together. Jeff thought she was still getting married to Stuart, that today was her wedding day! She recalled Stuart's offhand invitation to Jeff and his mother after Andrew's birth. No one had thought to inform them of the change in plans, so now Jeff believed he was interrupting her wedding. She felt a huge bubble of laughter building in the base of her chest. She looked up at him, trying desperately to swallow a smile.

"You kidnapped me from my own wedding?"

He winced. "I'd rather think of it as a rescue. But yes, technically I'm kidnapping you. I know it's illegal, and probably unforgivable, but I'm a desperate man." He pulled another deck chair over to face her and sat down. "Look, I'm only going to keep you here long enough to present my case. If you still want to get married after I say what I have to say, then I'll take you back. No questions asked."

"What do you have to say?" Her eyes danced.

He took a deep breath. "That you're marrying the wrong man."

"I am?"

He nodded solemnly. "This is going to sound selfish, but I don't want you marrying Stuart. Or anyone. I love you, Chelsea. Just being close to you lights me up in a way I've never felt before."

She couldn't contain her laughter any longer; it burst out of her in a storm of giggles.

"What's so funny?" He drew back in his chair. "Believe me, I'm not joking."

She shook her head, trying desperately to get control of herself. "It isn't what you said," she gasped. "It's just that . . ." She collapsed again into helpless giggles.

He was frowning when she finally collected herself. Even then she had to wipe the tears out of her eyes and take several deep breaths before she could speak. "You didn't rescue me from my wedding, Jeff."

"What do you mean, I didn't rescue you? You were all dressed up in white, carrying a big bouquet of flowers—" His eyes widened. "Are you saying that the ceremony is already over?"

She shook her head. "No, I'm saying there isn't any ceremony. Today or any day. I broke the engagement with Stuart two weeks ago."

His jaw dropped. It took him a moment to speak. "You mean, there wasn't going to be any wedding?"

"That's right."

"But I saw the cars, the people—"

"We're holding a get-well party for Stuart's father."

He stared at her, a flush of embarrassment climbing his cheeks. "I'm sorry. I guess I owe you an apology."

"No, you don't." She shifted toward him, unconsciously fingering the shell that hung around her neck. "It's okay, really. I'm sorry I laughed."

He got to his feet. "I'll take you back right away. Your friends are probably wondering where you are." His glance shifted to the shell. "What's that?"

"It's the present you gave me on Eagle Island. Remember?"

"You saved it?"

"Of course. I haven't been able to get you out of my mind either." She smiled up at him. "Or my heart," she added softly.

"Chelsea," he whispered. "My darling." He took her hands and drew her up into his arms. He kissed her passionately, a long, ardent kiss, which seemed deliciously endless, until a dark thought teased the back of Chelsea's mind. She gently pulled away.

"What about your mother? She doesn't want you to have anything to do with me."

"I'm frankly not interested in her opinions, if it means I can't see you."

"But she threatened to cut off your inheritance."

"I'll have to take that chance. I can't live my life pursuing someone else's dreams." He smiled and touched the tip of her nose. "A wise person once told me that."

She smiled sheepishly. "I think I was really saying it to myself."

"But it does apply to me. My mother likes to play the autocrat, but no tyrant can rule without the people's consent. It was past time for a revolution."

"Did you quarrel with her?"

"I simply stated the facts. I told her who I was and

that, no matter how much I loved her, I couldn't live any life but my own."

"Is she furious?"

"More frightened than anything, I think. She's terrified of being left alone."

"Are you going back to Africa?"

He shook his head. "Not right away. Actually, I've been asked to join a practice in Portland. There's a lot of third-world poverty right in this area, and some local physicians feel they'd benefit from my experience." He smiled. "I have to admit, it's tempting. Ever since I met you, southern Maine's seemed just this side of paradise."

She swallowed. "I can't believe your mother's going to stop trying to control you. I know what she did to Brandon; I know how strong she is—" Her voice broke off as his expression saddened.

"If she was ever strong, she isn't now. She's not going to have the time or energy to interfere in her sons' lives anymore, I'm afraid. They've diagnosed her condition as multiple sclerosis."

"Oh, Jeff, I'm so sorry." Chelsea touched his cheek. "You know, the funny thing is, I like her. Maybe it's because of the way she helped Lori, but I feel kind of close to her, like she's somebody I respect and could even enjoy being with sometimes. Is there anything I can do to help?"

He shook his head. "She's getting the medical and emotional support she needs. And she seems more stable now that she knows what she's dealing with."

"Maybe you should throw a get-well party for her."

"That's a good idea." He grinned. "As long as Strawberry Lace does the catering."

"You bet. We can't afford to turn down a job offer."

"That reminds me: I want to make an investment in your company. I'm convinced that it could be a major force in the New England catering industry."

She laughed. "That's stretching it a bit. Have you forgotten that we're a two-person operation? Actually, more like one and a half right now."

"That's only temporary. With increased financial backing, you could expand to compete with the big Boston outfits."

"Financial backing?"

He smiled. "I may not have my inheritance yet, but I've set aside a sizable amount of money. Brandon's been telling me for years I should be on the lookout for a good investment."

She gazed into his eyes. "I can't believe this is really happening."

"There is one stipulation," he said solemnly. "You're going to have to make time in your schedule for a serious courtship."

"Courtship?" Her voice was faint.

He took her face between his hands. "I intend to pursue my own dreams from now on, Chelsea. And my first dream is making you my wife." He kissed her again, softly at first, and then more insistently, wrapping his arms around her and drawing her tightly against him.

She returned his kiss eagerly, pressing her body against his, running her hands up the firm column of his neck to stroke the soft, dark hairs that curled there. She was dimly conscious of the cry of a sea gull high above her and the sound of the waves licking the boat's hull. When he finally released her, she had to sit down again, to stop the dizzy spin that whirled through her whole body.

"Well," he said, his smile deepening slowly, so that the long dimple appeared in his left cheek, "if I'd known this rescue operation would be so successful, I'd have stowed some champagne on board. I feel like celebrating."

"So do I." Chelsea grinned up at him. "And I know where there's a great party. Complete with wonderful people and good dance music, and it's catered by the best service on the coast of Maine."

He laughed. "I'll take you back, on one condition."

"What's that?"

"That you save all your dances for me."

"It's a deal."

Jeff started the boat's engine and swung the bow around to head back to Bryant's Cove. Chelsea was certain she could already hear the sound of music, rolling toward them in three-quarter time across the sparkling water.